LAST THREE

EMMA LAST SERIES: BOOK THREE

MARY STONE

Copyright © 2023 by Mary Stone Publishing

All rights reserved.

No part of this book may be reproduced in any form or by any electronic or mechanical means, including information storage and retrieval systems, without written permission from the author, except for the use of brief quotations in a book review.

❀ Created with Vellum

This book is dedicated to those who have loved fiercely and lost deeply. May your journey lead you to peace.

DESCRIPTION

Three severed heads. Two worlds. One forbidden love.

Decapitated bodies seem to be following Special Agent Emma Last. First, it was the haunting appearance of the ghost of Ned, the late brother of Emma's friend and colleague, who was beheaded in a car accident years ago. Now, D.C.'s Violent Crimes Unit has two more headless victims.

Or is it four?

Over two eerie nights, a crypt raider exchanged ancient skeletal skulls for the freshly severed heads of two unidentified men. Yet, the whereabouts of their bodies and the stolen bones remain shrouded in mystery.

The why behind the seemingly ritualist crimes is even more perplexing. The victims have nothing in common other than age and orientation. But without their bodies, the cause of their deaths remains elusive.

Could Emma and her team be dealing with some type of dark occult practice? More importantly, is there a method to the killer's madness? The clock is ticking. And if bad things come in threes, Emma and the team only have one more day to decipher the mind of a killer before they strike again.

Last Three, the third book in the gripping new FBI series by bestselling author Mary Stone, reveals a horrifying glimpse into a killer's mind...and the fine line between love insanity, and the darkest corners of the human psyche.

1

Terry Derby swallowed as he took in the picture-perfect cabin on the lake. Frosted shrubs and pavers led to the front porch, where a welcome wreath hung on the door. Everything about the place was neatly maintained. The wooden exterior showed no signs of drooping. Windows twinkled as the winter sunlight waved its last goodbye across the horizon. He inhaled the scent of pines and woodsmoke.

When he reached the door, he gripped the hem of his button-down and tugged, smoothing the cloth over his slight belly, feeling a bit self-conscious.

Of course my perfect date lives in a perfect landscape. Talk about being out of my league.

But that didn't mean he wouldn't shoot his shot. Before he could break out in a cold sweat or freeze in the Maryland twilight, he steeled himself and rang the bell.

Tonight could be the night. This could be the night he got past his ex-wife for good. The night he made a new future—a *real* future—with a good woman.

A better woman than his ex.

Holly swung the door open, letting out a blast of warm

air. Her rosy-red lips widened into a big smile. "Terry, come in before you freeze!"

Terry stomped his boots on the porch mat and stepped inside. He leaned down to give her a quick *keep it friendly for now* hug. "You're just as beautiful as I remember. It's so good to see you again."

"Oh, you flirt." The jest bubbled from her throat in a singsong. Her blue eyes twinkled at him. Just like at the store, her understated makeup—except for those red, red lips—made his whole chest thrum. Even in a burlap sack, she'd have been gorgeous. "Come on back to the kitchen. I'll have dinner up soon. I hope you like lasagna?"

"I love it. And it smells great." Not a lie either. Her place smelled like an Italian restaurant full of pasta and garlic, and he couldn't have been happier.

Not a bad start for a guy who hasn't been on a date in a decade.

"I should've asked you over sooner." She fussed with the two place settings at the kitchen table. "I was so nervous. You understand? I'm just so glad you could make it tonight."

"Nowhere I'd rather be." He waved toward her stainless steel stove. "Anything I can help with? I'm glad to be useful."

Holly pulled her long brown hair around one shoulder and smoothed it down over her dress. The strands shimmered, even in the dim light. She then handed him a bottle of merlot. "Open the wine and relax?"

He took the bottle and corkscrew she offered. "You have a lovely place."

The buzzer on the oven dinged, pulling her attention. "A far cry from where we met anyway. But I couldn't have picked a better person to help me out there."

True enough. What single man didn't go into a hardware store hoping that a gorgeous woman would ask for help with some DIY project? He'd won the lottery that day.

From the moment Holly had asked if he knew anything

about nails, the whole scene had felt like a dream. Telling her he was a carpenter had been the start of a fifteen-minute conversation ending in exchanging business cards. And he'd been smooth in his closing too…simple and sweet. *"Just in case you need help with any other projects."*

Right.

Finally, two weeks and endless late-night phone calls later, she'd invited him over for dinner. He hated to ditch his kids for even one night, but Aaron and Lindsay were capable teenagers. Besides, they'd been telling him to go out and meet someone for months.

Maybe he owed it to himself, like they'd said. Either way…talk about a *someone* to open up his dating life again. This woman was the whole package, swaying around her kitchen on light feet, making his imagination swoon.

Settle down. It's one date. One night away from the kids. Keep cool.

Holly added a casserole dish of lasagna to the table just as he finished pouring their wine. She lit a single tall scarlet candle between them.

He tugged out her chair for her.

"Let me serve you?" As she leaned forward, her breasts nudged together beneath her low-cut blouse.

Terry's heart just about blew up. His mouth went dry. After so many months of it just being him and the kids, he didn't know how to process his luck. His first date out of the proverbial gate was with a dynamite brunette. There had to be a word better than "lucky" to describe what had happened.

Fate? Destiny?

Holly Watts was the most beautiful woman he'd ever met. Way prettier than his ex-wife. Inside and out. And if the smells at this table were any indication of taste, she was a damned good cook too.

Janet used to burn slow-cooked meals.

Portioning out healthy helpings of lasagna onto both their plates, Holly gave him a sweet smile. When she bit her lower lip, betraying her own nerves, his heart sped up in response. Maybe this night was about a lot more than lasagna for both of them.

I don't know what she sees in me. A middle-aged guy whose wife left him for her personal trainer. But damn, if I'm not excited to try to make this into something.

"Eat!" She gestured at his plate, dimples returning to her cheeks.

Terry picked up his knife and cut into the gooey lasagna. He lifted his fork and admired the gorgeous layers of cheese and meat and sauce. His mouth watered for it, as well as for the woman across from him.

Holly sipped her wine and watched as he wrapped cheese around his fork. "I love seeing someone enjoy my cooking."

He grinned, obliging her by taking his first, delicious bite. The flavor was deep and rich. Groaning in satisfaction, he closed his eyes in appreciation. He'd always been a big fan of garlic, and the dish delivered. This woman could cook.

With the second bite, more meat than cheese, he tasted a bit of nuttiness. Strange, but not unpleasant.

Terry swallowed a third bite, heavier on the interesting aftertaste.

Holly took a large bite of a piece of garlic bread.

"This is great. And unique. You must use a special blend of spices…?"

Her eyes crinkled, smiling, but he couldn't quite return the smile.

His lips tingled, feeling thick.

Then came the burning.

Am I allergic to something?

His fork fell from his hand, bounced off his new khakis—

leaving a sauce stain on its way down—and clattered to the floor.

"My hands…they're numb," he stammered, the words breaking up even as they formed.

As he tried to push back from the table, his limbs became useless lumps of wood, heavy and unwieldy. His chest tightened, and his heart pumped wilder as he stared across the table.

He was having a heart attack. He had to be.

Holly turned her head sideways, as if she were looking at someone else. "What do you think, honey? It's working, isn't it?"

Who was she talking to? *He* needed help.

Words still wouldn't come to him as his heart hammered louder.

Holly peered into thin air, everywhere but at him, as his gut rumbled and numbness spread up his arms and down through his legs.

The only damn thing that wasn't numb was his blasted, blasting heart.

Terry shut his eyes, gasping for a deeper breath against the pain of his pounding chest, but he couldn't quite bring air into his lungs. Sporadic thumps of muscle came as his heart hammered against his ribs. He felt himself spiraling, dizzy and hot.

When he fell sideways, the silver fork that he'd dropped poked hard into his back.

Holly stood. She seemed calm above him. Her bright-red lips formed a flat, thoughtful line as she studied him closely.

And then she said something, but not to him. Maybe to herself. Gibberish to his brain, though, which couldn't make sense of the situation.

Numb as his arms and legs, his thoughts spun in circles, sticking on the same little detail—Holly's calm, easy manner.

And then, she smiled.

His heartbeat sputtered, threatening to stop, and he gasped, trying to take in the still air of the kitchen. He clutched at his chest, which was working to split apart with a blasting slam of pain.

Aaron. Lindsay.

His children's faces flashed through his mind. The moments of their birth, bright red and screaming. Grabbing his hand as they crossed the street. The look in their eyes as he read them stories. Their expression of hope as he left their home earlier that night.

I'm sorry.

Try as he might to hold onto the image of their beautiful faces, Holly's blue eyes were the last thing he saw before he closed his own.

This is my last first date.

2

As FBI Special Agent Emma Last jogged along the side of her apartment building, she skirted an overflowing trash can and an untrimmed tree.

Ah, the joys of city life.

At the end of the block, she skidded to a stop.

To anyone else, the man walking toward her would seem normal in his checkered button-down shirt and gray chinos. His balding head was shiny, and his gray mustache was full. A small smile graced his lips. He swung a wooden cane jauntily. He'd seem "normal," anyway, if they could see him at all.

His white eyes stared both at her and at nothing. He grunted as she reached the corner.

Air plumed from her lips, clear in the streetlight, but the natural cold was no match for the icy chill surrounding the ghost. Rather than acknowledge him, Emma turned on her heel and jogged back the way she'd come, circling the building to the back entrance. Going in this way meant using her key card three times, instead of just once at the entrance, to get through the various security measures and gates, but that was fine.

She slowed down on the icy sidewalk between the security gate and her building before using her card to finally get back into the relative warmth.

Even if her sanity wasn't quite *that close* to breaking, the fear of going crazy was real.

Earlier that day, Ned Logan, the late brother of her colleague Special Agent Mia Logan, had paid her a white-eyed visit too.

What a day.

"Ghost overload." The elevator was empty, so her voice sounded loud. But maybe it would scare any nearby spirits away. Couldn't hurt to try. "That's right. I'm going to shower and go to bed. Leave me alone."

Or maybe it's time to take real action, Emma girl.

She'd never believed in psychics or ghost hunters. As someone who'd taken multiple classes and trainings on human behavior, she knew discovering secrets was often just a matter of observation.

Now, knowing what she'd seen, she wondered if maybe there was something to it. After all, she'd had coffee with Mrs. Kellerly nearly every day. If ghosts were real, some of the spiritualists must've been on to something.

After Esther, the fortune teller at the Ruby Red Spectacle Circus, warned her of the Other, Emma realized she might not be alone...even if the encounter had made her distinctly uncomfortable.

Speeding through a shower, Emma stayed in her bedroom only long enough to throw on jeans and a sweatshirt. She barely glanced at her mom's photo, but the thing vibrated at her, nabbing her attention anyway.

That was a relatively new development.

The photo wasn't falling over like it did before. Now it shook if she looked at it, all but rattling on the nightstand.

When it shuddered the first time, Emma tried to stare the

picture down, thinking a force of will might make it stop. The frame had just rattled harder, so much that she couldn't make out her mother's features. Normally, it was easy to see Gina Last's smile as she danced with infant Emma. Lately, her mother's blue eyes became blurry swirls whenever the picture started trembling.

Not exactly an improvement on the situation.

In the kitchen, Emma wasted no time in flipping open her laptop. Part of being smart meant knowing when to ask for help…and she needed help.

Now, she just needed to find a psychic who wasn't a whackjob.

Apparently, finding a non-whackjob was no easy task. Site after sketchy site appeared in her browser. Over-the-top crystal ball hawkers, tarot advertisements, and psychic testimonials. *Life-changing predictions! Accurate readings!*

She'd reached the third page of her Google search when she spotted someone who seemed promising.

Marigold Florence's site was unassuming. Simple background colors and clear fonts made everything easy to read. No flashing banners or *Click Here Now!* ads. The site could've been advertising antique sales based on the feel of the web page alone. Only a simple explanation of services told the supernatural tale. A brief biography listed Marigold's bona fide training with another psychic.

All of which sounded great, Emma supposed. Nothing stood out as particularly helpful, however.

She nearly gasped when she read, *Provides connections with the Other*.

Out of all the sites she'd explored so far, Marigold's was the only one that referenced "the Other."

This was the person she needed.

In seconds, heart beating fast, Emma typed up an email, requesting an appointment, and hit send.

Stretching her arms above her, she released a sigh before moving to her fridge to find something with electrolytes in it. While rehydrating, she stared at her computer.

What was she supposed to do now?

Marigold could take hours or maybe days to respond. If the psychic didn't get back to her soon, Emma might find herself drowning in ghosts. Looking through more websites seemed like a wasted effort.

Ping.

"Wow."

Emma collapsed back onto the stool at her island and stared at her email.

Marigold had already responded.

Emma, it's great to hear from you, and I'd love to help if I can. I'm actually available tonight if you can make it over prior to 9:00 p.m., when I'm expecting another client. If not, perhaps tomorrow night between 7:00 p.m. and 10:00 p.m.? Just let me know, and I'll look forward to seeing you. Feel free to just come on by if you're free tonight.

Emma's stove clock read seven twenty.

Damn right she could make that work.

Marigold's address was included in the email's closing salutation, and Emma was glad and a bit disturbed to realize it wasn't more than a five-minute drive from her apartment.

No time like the present.

Grabbing her coat, Emma headed out and down the stairs. At her car, she slammed the driver's side door behind her—even though physical barriers hadn't stopped a single ghost yet—and immediately locked herself in. The effort made her feel better.

She flew through the parking lot fast enough to raise the eyebrows of Bobby the security guard, the one living person strolling down the sidewalk.

"Trust me when I say it's an emergency!" Emma hollered out the window as his eyes widened.

"Slow down and get there in one piece!" Bobby called after her as she peeled out of the lot and down the street.

She smiled, took a deep breath, and slowed, eyeing street signs.

Marigold's house stood out only because of its warm blue hue among endless blocks of brick and neutral-colored homes.

She had no signage, though. Only a neat placard with Marigold's name and contact information, placed just beside the door, spoke to the fact that the woman ran a business of some kind out of her home.

Emma appreciated the subtlety. She lifted the knocker just as the lock snicked open. Immediately, she dropped it and stepped back, her heart speeding up. Maybe this would be the night she'd finally learn something about the Other.

"Emma Last?"

"That's me." Emma willed her hands to stop sweating. She hadn't been this nervous around axe murderers, if her last case was any measure. "Marigold?"

Smiling, the woman waved her inside, opening the door wide.

Emma stepped inside, and Marigold closed the door behind her. The home was normal, with nice oversize, microsuede furniture and a fireplace burning brightly. Family pictures hung from the walls. Deep-gold curtains were tied neatly, framing the view of brick homes outside. It was utterly and unquestionably normal.

Just like the unassuming woman who'd opened the door.

Marigold's warm brown eyes and straight brown hair seemed designed to counter any stereotype associated with "psychic." With no bandanas or huge hoop earrings in sight, Marigold wore a modest, knee-length skirt and a floral blouse. She didn't look the sixty-two years of age that was listed on the website. Emma would've guessed somewhere in her forties...but maybe that was the dyed hair talking.

"Not what you expected?" The woman grinned as she locked her front door.

Emma's face warmed. Marigold was clearly used to her reaction. "Better than expected," she said honestly.

Marigold beamed. "Well, let's not waste any time. Follow me."

She led Emma past the living room and into a side room with dark, built-in cabinets and a china cabinet full of books. She poured tea into two mugs from a sideboard and set the steaming drinks down on a center table. Simple and wooden. Unassuming, like the pretty woman who'd set up the space.

Aside from an old-fashioned quilt hanging on one wall, the only decor was a flat, square dish sitting on the table, off to the side. Crystal blue, full of water, with flower petals floating on the surface.

As New Agey decorations went, it wasn't much. Marigold's minimal setup struck Emma as oddly powerful. For a few seconds, she couldn't tear her eyes away from the bowl.

Marigold swirled the water with one finger, setting the flower petals to twirling. She brought Emma back to the present with one quiet question.

"Now, my dear, what type of otherworldly problems are you having?"

The simplicity of the question made Emma's hands freeze around her steaming mug.

She'd been longing to speak to someone about this for a while. Holding it in, knowing no one would really understand, had weighed on her. She could finally talk it out, ask questions, and learn. A relieved laugh bubbled out of her throat, and Marigold only smiled back at her.

Marigold radiated patience as Emma gathered herself.

But Emma didn't need patience. She needed answers. So she tamped down the laughter and dug in.

"It started when I was in Ireland. Almost four years ago." Emma swallowed, forcing herself to slow down and take a breath. "I saw a bone-thin woman standing on a cliff. At the time, I wasn't sure she was real, but she was, well, she might've been my first…encounter with a ghost. With the Other."

Marigold tilted her head, resembling a curious puppy. "What do you mean by *might've* been?"

"There was a moment, in high school. I had a conversation with a…boy. At first, I didn't think anything of it. I'd had trouble with him, and he said something rude the night of graduation, at a party."

"Trouble" didn't quite cut it. She'd intervened when Brad Caits was assaulting her friend Sophie, back in the fall of their senior year. Brad was an entitled jerk with very few redeeming qualities. The son of two Hollywood powerhouses, he exemplified "privilege" and abused his status and parentage to get his way.

Stopping him and being there for Sophie through the healing process started Emma on her mission to help others. Why that douche had to be her first ghostly encounter was still a mystery, one she often chose to forget.

"The next morning, on the news, I heard he'd died in a car wreck. So I couldn't have spoken to him. But I did."

"Of course you did." There was no hint of mockery in Marigold's voice, only a matter-of-fact tone that Emma found reassuring.

Leaning forward over the little table, Emma fought the rush of emotion back down her throat. "You have no idea what it feels like to finally…admit that. Say it out loud."

The woman's eyes went soft. "I could tell you needed to

speak when you sent that email. I'd been waiting for someone who needed me to get in touch today. I'm here to help."

Thank you. Thank you, thank you, thank you, thank you.

Trying to pull together her thoughts, Emma could only nod. The woman could have said—probably *did* say—that to everyone, but her words had the ring of truth. Emma had come too far now. There was nothing to do but trust her.

"But that woman in Ireland was really the start of things." Emma closed her eyes, thinking back to the Irish ghost floating along beside her. Clearly dead and speaking to her and nobody else. "But I've continued to see them ever since…"

Once Emma got going, she found herself spewing out her story like word vomit, fast and free, all the details stored up for just this moment.

Marigold was the picture of patience as she listened through the recitation of Emma describing ghost after ghost, encounter after encounter. The hair had raised on Emma's arms as she told of how so many ghosts had warned her that "they" didn't like her in the Other. How ghosts had sometimes nudged her toward clues in cases. How at other times, they ignored her entirely. How sometimes, they mocked her.

She told Marigold how her colleague's dead brother had found her just that morning, seeking her out, leaning his translucent head—Ned had been decapitated in the car wreck that took his life—near her car window. She'd sped away like a bat out of hell, overwhelmed and panicked.

And her mother's picture, which had been constantly falling over on its own, now vibrated every time she looked at it.

"And your mother died…" Marigold prodded.

"When I was two." Emma wrapped her hands tighter

around the mug. The porcelain had cooled as she spoke. "From a brain tumor."

Marigold's forehead creased in sympathy.

Emma didn't tell her that her father was also gone, or that she'd had a less-than-close relationship with him. That didn't feel pertinent, and anyway, she guessed the woman knew as much already.

"There's a message related to the picture, I'm sure of it." Emma steadied herself, watching Marigold for any reaction. Would the psychic think she was crazy? "I just have no idea what that message is. And I don't know why my mother won't simply appear and talk to me like all the other ghosts."

Though there was no chill in the air, Marigold rubbed her hands together. "I'm guessing that's not an easy answer, Emma, but I hope we'll come to find it. Have there been clearer messages?"

"I don't know about *clearer*. But there've been some direct messages. A couple weeks ago, we were working a case at a circus—"

"The Ruby Red Spectacle Circus? I saw that on the news."

"Yes, that one. A circus fortune teller, Esther, said that forces are…are gathering against me."

"That must've been difficult to hear."

Difficult to hear was an understatement. Confusing, terrifying, *lonely*—if she allowed herself to define her feelings, because she couldn't tell a soul about any of this—those would just barely scratch the surface. For starters, who would believe her?

Emma hoped Marigold would. The psychic's accepting brown eyes encouraged her to say more.

"Esther said that if I'm very quiet, very still, I'll sense the ghosts coming. She mentioned a wolf, also. She said that the path to the wolf is covered in innocent blood, but that it's the path I have to take."

Marigold leaned forward, focused. "The path to the wolf is covered in innocent blood? That's what she said?"

Emma forced herself to sip at the lukewarm tea. The beverage didn't help her nerves but relaxed her throat enough to answer. "Yes, that's what she said."

Marigold waved one hand. "And did you ask her what she meant?"

"She didn't know." The frustration of that night came right back to haunt Emma. She'd just captured a killer, barely saving a young woman in the process. Then, she'd been accosted by a fortune teller who wouldn't explain anything. "And she didn't exactly stay around to chat."

"Well." Marigold stood and went to the side table, hitting the start button on the electric kettle. "That doesn't surprise me, I guess."

"Why doesn't it surprise you?"

"The Other, the afterlife, for all intents and purposes, is a mysterious, cryptic place."

That meant Marigold didn't know either. Though that shouldn't have surprised Emma, the realization still left a hollow feeling in her gut.

All her life, Emma fought to be the best. She was determined to be independent and prepared for anything. If she didn't know the answers to a problem, she would know how to find them. Her focus helped her solve mysteries and fix whatever went wrong.

The whole damn situation she'd found herself in was foreign and added more and more anxiety with each passing day.

If someone like Marigold, who'd trained herself to be comfortable with the supernatural, couldn't offer up answers, who could?

"I need help." Emma hadn't meant to say that. Not out loud.

Marigold reached across the table, her fingers resting near Emma's but not quite touching them. "Some curses are gifts, and some gifts are curses. From what you've described, I believe you've received both gifts and curses. Likely from different sources. I can help you understand why you have this power, Emma. But...you have to understand that only you can confront the source."

Emma's heart picked up speed. "You mean...face the source, as in...face the wolf? One and the same?"

Marigold's lips lifted in a tiny smile that appeared more sad than comforting. "I can't be sure of anything yet, but perhaps."

Emma couldn't quite hide her disappointment that more answers weren't forthcoming.

The psychic grasped Emma's forearm. "It's okay, Emma girl. We'll figure this out together."

Emma girl? How does she know that's what I call myself?

Marigold gave her arm a gentle squeeze of reassurance, and despite the oddity of her words, Emma's heart was infused with a spark of hope.

3

Shifting his laptop screen for better reading, Special Agent Leo Ambrose sipped a beer and set the can back down on the table beside his couch. Refreshing as the ice-cold beverage was, it couldn't quite settle his nerves.

Much earlier, he'd intended to relax with some reruns, but he'd fallen asleep in front of the television and started dreaming about wolves instead. He couldn't remember the dreams when he jolted awake with sweat beading on his forehead, just the subjects of them.

If he was going to jump like a scared kitten every time he dreamed of the damned animals—which was apparently every night now—he damn sure wanted to know what he was jumping about.

And so, he sat, after nine on a Sunday night, researching wolves like some sixth grader getting ready for a zoology presentation. Across from him, a cozy fire crackled below his flat-screen. But the warmth didn't do much to calm his anxiety.

An hour ago, he'd sought the facts and only the facts on

the wild lupines. He'd long since spiraled down an internet hole into the spiritual symbolism of wolves.

And the research was getting him nowhere.

Ghostly predators.

Representing commitment to family because of their pack mentality.

Great communication among members of a pack.

He could've come up with the same bullshit off the cuff. *Stupid internet.*

Leo swallowed another sip of beer and muttered at his screen. "I'm a friggin' FBI agent. I'm trained to see everyone as a wolf in sheep's clothing until they prove otherwise." He took a longer gulp. "Maybe it's the other way around. Innocent until proven guilty means everyone's a sheep until they're proven to be a wolf."

Maybe beer and internet rabbit holes weren't the best way to spend a Sunday night.

He tore his eyes away from the laptop and flicked on the television again, rolling through channels, hoping something would catch his interest. Something, anything other than wolves.

I don't even know why I'm letting myself get so worked up about this wolf thing.

He hated this kind of fake spiritualism crap.

Symbolism of wolves, his ass. The whole thing freaked him out and reminded him of the creepy religious stuff Yaya, his grandmother, always had around, all candles and superstitions.

But it would be easier to try to walk off the wolf references if it weren't for fellow FBI Special Agent Emma Last. More and more, he felt like he was catching on to something that her other colleagues were missing altogether. Maybe not Mia, but the rest of them, for sure.

During the Ruby Red Spectacle Circus case, he'd caught

Emma staring off into space, like she was seeing something no one else could. She talked down the killer knowing things she shouldn't have known. And he could've sworn she'd been talking to herself...or someone...at the close of the Little Clementine case, even though there'd been nobody around.

Emma Last was different. And he wasn't quite sure whether it was a good or bad type of "off." Not yet. Not without learning quite a bit more.

A loud knock at the door startled Leo, and he barely managed to catch his laptop before it crashed onto the coffee table. He contemplated grabbing his gun but decided against it. Criminals didn't usually knock.

When he peered through the peephole, his colleague Denae Monroe grinned back. His breath caught for a split second. He'd enjoyed their recent dinner together and hoped she was here for him and not for business. He quickly checked his phone for a message from their supervisor. No text notifications anywhere on the screen. That meant she was here for pleasure.

When he opened the door, her natural curls waved in the wind. "Can I come in?"

"Of course." He stepped back. "Want a beer?"

"Uh...yeah, thanks." She hesitated in the foyer, her gaze catching the sweater she'd left in his truck the night before, now laid over an armchair. Leo followed her line of sight.

Shit, right. That's the only reason she came by.

"Unless you have to leave?"

She shrugged, that smile he was starting to enjoy more and more slipping back onto her lips. "No, I've got time. I just didn't want to impose. I thought I'd be able to stop by this afternoon, but the day got away from me."

"No imposition." He dipped into his kitchen and came out with two beers, opening both and handing one to her. "My family and friends are in Iowa and Miami, remember? It's nice to have someone stop in."

She primped some of her curls as if she were a glamourous actress. "Anyone at all, huh? Just so you're not alone with your thoughts?"

Leo tried to hide his blush with a swig from his beer. "Not anyone. Someone. Uh, you. That's what I mean. By someone."

He wasn't sure when he'd lost his powers of speech, but he hoped they returned sometime in the next two seconds.

Get it together.

Denae giggled, which struck him as adorable because she wasn't the giggling type. She set down her beer to take off her coat. He plucked the garment from her fingers and laid it across the armchair with her sweater.

They moved to the living room, and he sat on the couch. She plopped down beside him.

Right beside him.

"You gonna put your arm around me or not, Scruffy?" She brushed an errant curl away from his face. The friendly—yet intimate—gesture sent tingles down the back of his neck. "Offering a woman a beer means you'd like to, right?"

Somehow he managed not to spill his beer all over her.

He set his arm against the back of the couch, and his hand, ever so hesitantly, rested on her shoulder.

Denae grabbed the remote control and flicked off the TV. "The fire's nice," she murmured, settling against his side.

"So's this." Talk about an understatement. Denae's body fit against his perfectly, and he'd never have guessed that her curves would feel this soft up close. The weave of her expensive sweater had nothing on this woman's ability to generate warmth.

"I'm glad you came over." Finally, he'd stopped stammering.

She laid her head against his shoulder and sipped her

beer. "Had to make sure you didn't forget about me after a whole day apart, right? And you did say I could come by for the sweater."

"I did." His voice came out huskier than he intended, and he coughed to hide it. "So, uh, you had plans with family today?"

"My little brother was passing through town. He was nice enough to grab us tickets to the Capitals game this afternoon." She snorted. "Not like I could turn that down, and we ended up having a long dinner downtown. He's got girl troubles, unlike you." She nudged him with an elbow.

"Feels like I'm the lucky one, then." Leo took a long drink, wondering why the alcohol hadn't gotten him past the awkward teenager phase. This was his third, after all. "Is he at your place?"

"Nah, he's crashing at a friend's. And what about you? You have siblings?"

"Three brothers. We were raised by my grandmother and my grandfather. Me and my brothers call her Yaya. Papu, my grandfather…died in an accident, so it's just her and my brothers back in Iowa."

"Multiple Ambrose brothers? They must have had their hands full. I'm sorry to hear about your parents and your grandfather, though."

"Yeah…it was a long time ago." Leo turned his attention back to his beer, working to keep his mind on the present. "But you'd like my brothers. Aleksy's big into hockey too."

Denae giggled again, the sound lightening a weight in his chest. "Yeah, well, I don't think I can handle taking care of more than one Ambrose. Let me guess, you're the youngest?"

"Hey, I resent that." He chanced rubbing his hand up and down her upper arm, enjoying the feel of her snuggling against him in response. "As I am an *older* brother."

Denae reached across him, setting her empty can on the

side table. She rested against him, one arm falling naturally over his chest as her head fit against his shoulder. "Too much too soon?" Her voice was almost a whisper, light and fast.

"Not at all." He leaned back, allowing his hand to keep roving up and down her arm. That was enough. Hell, it was enough just to have her there after such a stressful night. Such a stressful week.

She kept quiet and relaxed deeper against him. Tension seemed to drain out of them both, making him wonder if she'd had some family drama to deal with earlier. He respected her decision to stay quiet, if that was the case. Heaven knew he wasn't ready to divulge deep, dark secrets. All the better if she wasn't there yet either.

At least for now, his psychological plate was well and truly full. With a giant wolf sitting on top of it.

He'd take a pretty woman leaning against him as long as he could get it.

4

The weight of the sledgehammer felt good and right. The tool was a twenty-pounder I'd picked up new last week, just three days before my practice run. Busting into Sid Waller's crypt had roughed up the sledgehammer's head, wearing it in for the tasks I had planned. I'd struggled at first, slamming my way through the stone marking Sid Waller's final resting place. But the tool was seasoned now, like me.

I felt sure this would be the start of a glorious experience of work, labor, and toil, all for the glory of rebuilding what had been broken. Of rejoining what had been severed. I'd succeeded with Sid, proving to myself that not only could I perform the physical task of breaking into a crypt, but also that my ritual was sound.

But Sid had just been practice. Tonight, I would see how Marcus Peabody performed as the first of my ritual transformations.

"*Omne trium perfectum*, my dearest. Everything is perfect in threes." On those words, I raised the sledgehammer and swung.

The steel head struck the stone of the crypt, sending

vibrations up my arm. A heavy bit of stone chipped away from the facade of Marcus Peabody's memorial plating. Adjusting my safety goggles, I grinned and lifted the hammer for my second swing, aiming for the same spot as before. The head's solid metallic *thunk* echoed off the mausoleum walls.

At nearly two in the morning, nobody would notice me here. Van Der Beek Cemetery was a run-down inner-city graveyard surrounded by overgrown brush. Not a locked gate to be had. The mausoleum old man Peabody's family chose was in the very back.

I was so sure of being alone, in fact, I'd even turned the lights in the mausoleum on. One good thing about this sort of structure…no windows.

No, the only one to hear or see me was my dear dead husband, and Michael was the last one who'd interfere tonight.

My dearly departed leaned against a nearby crypt. He winked at me, giving me his blessing on this first step of our journey. I winked back as he moved a bit farther into the shadows, as if to give me room to work. Almost floating, like a good ghost should.

Another swing of the sledgehammer, the third, and the force of the hit set my whole upper body to shaking. The stone with Peabody's name was nothing but a chipped mess of granite now. Three strikes had been all it took to erase the inscription associating him with this crypt.

And now, Michael and I were free to make use of its contents for our purposes. Not that I would be completely destroying Marcus Peabody's corpse. His family didn't deserve that, any more than Michael and I deserved to be split apart the way we'd been.

The Peabody family would understand what I had to do, though. I was sure they would—at least, I hoped they would—if they ever learned the details. Once somebody found out what I'd done, the police would be called in, of course, but I had to believe they would refrain from sharing the facts of my ritual with the Peabody family.

And I imagined insurance would cover the replacement of the inscription stone.

Marcus Peabody's family deserved no less.

I began swinging my hammer again, chipping away at the sealed crypt containing the man's corpse. By all accounts, he had been a good man. His obituary waxed poetic about his family life. His children remembered him on their social media pages around Father's Day and other holidays. They posted cherished family photos and included heartwarming details about the man. One time, he'd rescued a box of puppies from the side of the road. At Christmas, he'd run a Toys for Tots drive.

Crap like that.

"He liked to bowl." I hauled the sledgehammer back for another blow as I spoke to Michael. "His league threw a wake for him after he died."

I put my full weight into this next swing, stumbling as the sledgehammer broke through.

"Pay dirt, baby." I winked in Michael's direction again and dropped the sledgehammer.

The Peabodys had placed Marcus in the second crypt up from the floor. I knelt to examine the opening I'd made. It was at a good height for me to work. I reached into my tool bag for the smaller sledgehammer, a three-pounder that would be perfect for knocking away the remaining stone. I worked with steady strikes, enlarging the opening so I could maneuver the casket out.

When the opening was big enough, I clenched the handle at the end of the box, gripping it as tightly as I could with my gloved hands.

"I hope this'll slide out easier than the last one."

I pulled.

Nothing.

I wiped sweat off my brow. Thank goodness the weather was chilly—I might've passed out if it were any warmer. Grave robbing was quite the workout.

Michael remained in the shadows where I couldn't see him clearly, but I knew he was there, watching me, willing me on to complete my task.

"Couldn't be that easy, could it, baby? But that's okay. I won't let us down."

From my bag, I pulled out the iron bar and one of the casters I'd brought. The bar took some work to wedge beneath the box, and I only had a few inches of space to work with, but I got it in eventually. Resting my weight on the end of the bar, I managed to lift the casket enough to set the caster beneath it at the front right corner.

The casters were mounted on metal plates that I'd rigged to grip the wood of a casket or coffin. Since I hadn't known which I'd be dealing with, I'd made sure to purchase casters sturdy enough to bear the weight of a casket.

Thankfully, I'd prepared well, roughing up the mounting plates on all three and bending them to stab into the wood like spikes. As I lowered the casket onto the first of them, I was pleased to see the jagged edges engage with the wood.

With the first caster in place, it was easier to slide the iron bar in deeper. I reached in and inserted a second caster toward the center of the box, about a foot back from the crypt opening.

Placing a third and final caster at the front left corner, I sat back to rest and examine my work so far.

Sweat collected on my back and my brow, and I wondered if Michael enjoyed the view. Maybe I wasn't a bodybuilder, but for a petite woman in my mid-forties, I was damn sure in peak physical condition.

Crouching in front of the crypt again, I grabbed the handle and yanked. The casket shifted enough that I could get a better grip now. It wasn't out yet...but I was getting there.

"This was a good man, baby." I rested for a moment with my hands on my knees, stretching out my lower back. "And he's a perfect fit for this spirit renewal, I promise. I've done good for you so far."

A good man was paramount for this venture, so I'd been careful. Michael deserved the best.

Mr. Peabody would put us on good footing.

The men I'd used for the practice ritual hadn't mattered. Those two had been bad news. The first man I'd killed, Jay South, had been a bartender. I'd gone into his so-called establishment thinking it would be a good place to find a man whose earthly presence wouldn't be missed.

I'd prepared a lasagna and had it ready to go at home. All I had to do was wait for him to arrive, if I did find a good target at the bar. Lo and behold, Jay had slapped a girl's ass right as I'd walked in. It'd been easy work to lure him home with promises of a warm meal and a warmer bed to follow.

With that one unseemly, disrespectful slap, Jay South had sealed his fate.

"Peabody wouldn't touch a woman like that." I tugged on the handle again, trying to angle the casket so I could roll it out.

I took a minute to catch my breath and meet my husband's eyes. He still looked as good as he had when he'd been alive. Blond and blue-eyed, with the best smile that only real family money could buy. He had a fantastic smile, and he gave it to me now with a thumbs-up. I wished I could hear his voice, but he rarely spoke. I guessed that required a lot of effort.

"Jay South was easy pickings, Michael. Just like Sid

Waller." I looked back at the crypt, gearing myself up for the next part. I'd come closest to hurting myself at this stage of the practice run last time. "Sid Waller was a thief and a drunk, but his crypt wasn't all that different from this one… just closer to South's bar."

Three.

I clamped my hands around the handle.

Two.

I braced my legs and visualized the casket coming out in one go.

One.

I yanked as hard as I could, sending the casket barreling through the crypt opening on its brand-new, yet loose, casters. I spun out of the way as the two casters I'd placed up front broke free and hit the floor right as the casket tilted. Momentum pulled the casket forward. It thundered through the opening, spitting out the third caster. Luckily, when it landed, I was on my ass a few feet away.

The coffin sat at an angle with the front propped up by the edge of the crypt.

"Good enough, right?"

Michael nodded, and I wiped sweat from my brow before standing up.

Grabbing the foot of the casket once more, I maneuvered it the rest of the way out, nearly turning my ankle on a caster. Breathing hard, I stepped around to the head, still propped up on the lip of its former resting place. Putting both hands on the box's top edge, I gave it all I had and shoved.

The casket fell with a ground-shaking *thud* that probably rocked every corpse in the mausoleum.

I collected the scattered casters and sledgehammers, thinking I'd be too amped up to remember them if I waited until the gruesome part of my task was done. Once the tools were back in my black duffel, I turned back to the casket.

Pulling on the lid didn't do any good, which meant it was sealed. So much for luck being on my side. But that was fine…good things didn't come easy, right? This eventuality was the whole reason I'd brought a hatchet to begin with.

The first strike splintered the wood, but the hollow thump revved me up. I'd intended to make three solid strikes, but after the second sent bits of wood flying, I lost my focus and became a woman possessed. Down the hatchet fell, rising only to be brought down once more. Hit after hit, splinters flew in my peripheral vision. I aimed at the front of the box. I only needed Marcus's head, after all.

When my hatchet blade sank between the wood fibers and became lodged in the lid, I sobbed out loud.

"Sweet relief is coming, Michael, it's coming. We're almost there."

I wrenched the hatchet free and gently used the blade to knock away the remaining bits of wood obscuring my target.

I'd expected a flood of foul odors, but what came out of the casket wasn't so bad. Dank, sour, unpleasant, and artificial…no different from the even older stink of Sid Waller's corpse, but not nearly so gag-inducing as the internet had led me to believe. Of course, Mr. Peabody had been well preserved.

The hatchet made fast work of the wood now that I'd gotten in. I sliced away the sides of the hole I'd made, enlarging it just as I'd enlarged the hole to his crypt earlier. Soon, Peabody's slightly shrunken—extremely dehydrated—but well-preserved head peeked up from the now oversize neck of a fancy black suit.

Michael grunted his approval from beside the crypt's gape-mouthed opening. I steeled my gut and hefted my little saw. Even though no blood would make a mess of my work, I didn't love this part. I also regretted my choice to use a manual saw instead of one of those cool bone saws. The mechanical saws just seemed like they'd be loud, and I wanted quiet.

"I've got this, baby. We're going to keep you close to me. Rejuvenate your spirit just like I promised. Maybe it's a struggle, but we'll get through it together. We'll get through it."

We had to. I was running out of time.

Swallowing down some bile, I settled the saw in place against Peabody's neck. I made the first stroke, feeling the blade catch and snag against the nearly mummified flesh. It became bound in his skin, so I dug in with real pressure on the backstroke. After that, I developed a rhythm that allowed me to regain some composure as I worked.

Soon, though, the saw blade was moving through Marcus Peabody's neck in fits and starts, becoming bound or snagged on almost every stroke. Getting through the skin and desiccated muscle was like sawing into rubber. I had to look away a few times, and slow down more than once, but I made sure my saw's placement remained true.

When I met bone, I had to take even more care to keep my saw in the cut and prevent the blade jumping out with a wild stroke. It was like trying to saw through rock, and my patience was running thin. I'd been in here making enough racket to wake the dead, and I couldn't risk being caught, not before I'd finished what I'd started.

And tonight was just the first of my efforts. Steadying my grip on the saw handle, I chanted my mantra in time with my strokes.

"Omne trium perfectum. Omne. Trium. Perfectum."

The smell eventually grew worse, just like with Sid Waller at Angel Willows Cemetery, but I endured it. For Michael.

I chanted and I sawed, and I chanted some more.

When I glanced down and found the head a few inches from the body, little bits of bone and fabric littering the casket's interior, an emotion akin to love cascaded over me.

I was done.

Slamming my hand down on the splintered lid, I allowed myself a laugh of celebration.

I wiped away some splinters with my glove. *Moment of truth time.* I reached down and gripped the old man by his hair. When I lifted his head, it came up easy, right through the opening.

Michael nodded, and happy tears welled in my eyes. "I told you I could do it, baby."

Relief flooded my system.

I wrapped Marcus Peabody's newly freed head in the red satin fabric I'd bought special for the occasion. That done, I pulled Michael's old bowling bag from my duffel and tucked my prize away. After discovering Peabody's love of bowling, the bag felt appropriate. Realizing the two men had something in common had made this process easier. Everything felt connected. Maybe Peabody's spirit would appreciate the gesture, if he was watching.

I put the bowling bag and its precious cargo in the black duffel, then pulled Terry Derby's head from its own satin sheath. A smear of lasagna sauce still stained Terry's lips. At least he'd enjoyed the first few bites of his last meal. Remembering the sounds of pleasure escaping his throat as he chewed, I almost felt sad about what I'd done.

But Terry had been a good man, as well, and I knew his spirit would be at rest, even if his final moments had been marked by intense agony.

Placing Terry Derby's head atop Marcus Peabody's body, inside his casket, I completed the first real step of the ritual. Soon, my Michael would come back to me. It was really happening. Somehow, placing Jay South's head atop Sid

Waller's body in Angel Willows Cemetery hadn't felt transformative. The spirits of both men had been lowly, and their earthly behavior had been foul. That must've been why I hadn't felt a rush of completion the way I did now. Staring down at Terry Derby's beautiful head, I knew this ritual would work.

I still had two more transformations to complete, and I felt a pang of fear that I might be caught before I'd succeeded. I paused to catch my breath and look around. The mausoleum was silent. No sirens wailed in the streets outside this old, forgotten cemetery. My work would not be interrupted, and I would complete my ritual in full, just as I'd dreamed of doing for these three long years without Michael by my side. I stood and regarded my work.

The sight inside the casket was macabre, and the mausoleum was simply a mess, just like the one I'd used for our practice run.

"It can't be helped." I zipped the duffel closed over Peabody's head and my tools. I sought out my husband's lurking form. "I don't think anyone will discover our work at Angel Willows, not anytime soon. That cemetery is so abandoned, but this one…"

Shrugging, I picked up my old coat from near the entrance and slipped into it. I examined the destruction we'd caused, shrugging again. Bending, I braced myself then hefted the heavy duffel onto my shoulder. Compared to the weight of Michael's death, it was nothing.

But thank goodness Michael had made me do all those push-ups over the three years since he'd been taken. He came to me every morning and every night, reminding me of the work I would have to accomplish, and the strength I would need to do it.

"I didn't see any security cameras, but that doesn't mean we won't be seen."

Michael's presence reassured me even though he didn't answer.

It's just three days. Three days is all we need, and then we hide. Together again, at last.

As I stepped over chips of broken stone, I remembered my ski mask. I yanked the fabric down over my head, making sure my long brown hair was tucked into the back of my long-sleeved t-shirt and underneath my coat. Man, but a shower was going to feel good. The splinters caught in my shirt and around my neck itched like hell.

"Either way, babe, we're fine. Nobody's going to know *I* was here."

At the mausoleum's entrance, I turned off the lights and gently opened the door, slipping out and closing it behind us. No point in drawing people's eyes needlessly to the crime scene.

With no cemetery gate to maneuver, I was back in my old Chevy within minutes.

Driving away, I did my best not to look at the intersection where Michael had been killed.

5

Emma jolted at the blaring of a car horn behind her but waited another two seconds to swerve—ever so slightly—to avoid taking her Prius through an elderly ghost with a cane.

Yes, she knew she didn't have to stop for ghosts in the crosswalk. She really, really did.

But driving through the old woman leaning on the cane was an exercise in brain chemistry gone wrong, and she hadn't had her coffee yet.

She'd slept pretty well after the consult with Marigold. Even finding her mother's picture face down that morning had garnered a tilt of her head instead of a curse. Somehow, she'd found someone to be in her corner where the ghosts were concerned, and two heads were better than one.

Or none.

As she pulled into the parking lot of the VCU offices, Emma spotted Ned Logan standing on the sidewalk. His body appeared solid, like all ghosts, but above his neck, there was only a translucent *appearance* of his head. This struck

Emma as more traditional. The kind of thing she'd seen in movies.

Normally, the only giveaway that a ghost *was* a ghost was the white eyes.

Ignoring him, she pulled into a parking spot.

Emma slumped in her seat even before she had the Prius turned off, hoping Ned wouldn't talk to her. By some miracle, she got her wish. When she looked up again, he was gone. She rushed inside.

When she reached her floor, Emma forced her gaze forward and made a beeline toward her desk, where she dropped her coat and bag before heading to the break room. The last thing she wanted was Ned Logan to be sitting at her desk when she got back.

She nearly skidded to a stop just outside the Violent Crime Unit's break room. Special Agent Mia Logan stood at the counter, opening a new canister of coffee creamer.

It seemed the Logan siblings were everywhere this morning.

If Emma had any luck at all, she hoped it would keep Ned Logan away…at least while his sister Mia was around. Emma had never in her life been good at hiding her emotions, and a coworker's dead brother would definitely tend to stir those pesky *feelings* up.

She steeled herself and slipped inside the break room.

Whatever luck she'd been banking on, it had run out. The air was icy cold.

Ned stood in front of the counter, staring at her. Emma couldn't get a mug without reaching through the headless man. And he knew it.

Even though Mia was in the room, Ned's phantom white eyes stared at Emma.

Emma tried to act normal. She tried. From the way Mia

looked at her, with an eyebrow raised and a puzzled smile on her lips, she was failing miserably.

Steeling herself, Emma reached through him—shivering at the sight of her arm sliding through the man's chest. She gagged a little as she poured herself some coffee. There was no resistance. No feeling of another person. Though the ghost did shiver, briefly making her wonder if he'd felt something.

Better not to go down that road, Emma girl. Just get your friggin' coffee and go.

"I need Mia. I don't know—"

She scowled at his translucent face as she stirred her coffee. "Me either." The under-her-breath mutter was a hair too loud, and Mia cleared her throat from a couple of feet away.

"You either what?"

Emma wanted to tell Ned to go away.

Mia's right here. The one real person in the room besides me. Can't he see her too?

Just as Emma turned back to Mia, working on some excuse for her behavior, Agent Vance Jessup swept into the room with a box of doughnuts. He flourished the sweets above him in a fashion that made Mia giggle like a schoolgirl. Emma laughed for their benefit.

To her relief, Ned Logan vanished.

"You okay?" Mia moved closer to Emma, her gaze concerned. "You look…off."

Emma bit down on her tongue, forcing herself to count to three rather than scream. Then she smiled, which she hoped seemed relaxed and casual. "I'm fine. Just…a weird morning. Doughnuts and coffee'll do the trick."

"Always." Vance passed Mia a cinnamon-iced doughnut then waved his hand over the selection. "What's your pleasure?"

Emma was about to decline, but the man was too chipper, his smile too big. Plus, she'd just said doughnuts would do the trick. He could see she was off her game too. A doughnut, it was. She was going to have to learn to force food down her throat even when ghosts stole her appetite. "I'll take a glazed. Thanks."

As the other agent turned back to choose one, Emma faced Mia's concerned expression…which turned into a deep frown when Emma jerked upright.

Not for no reason. Ned Logan had just reappeared behind his sister's shoulder. As bloody and headless as before.

Side by side, there was no mistaking the two siblings. Even with Mia in a suit and Ned in a bloodstained polo and khakis, their features were too similar to be mistaken for anything but brother and sister. Delicate, elfin features made them both look a decade younger than they were. In life, if not for Ned's shiny, dark-brown hair…they could have been twins.

Vance handed Emma her doughnut, which she bit into then dropped on the table as she fumbled her way from the room, nearly spilling her coffee in her haste to get out. Behind her, Vance asked if she was okay, while Mia tossed out the observation, "She seems ill. Like, pale."

I'll wash my face. I'll wash my face, down my coffee, wash my face again, and wake up from this nightmare. I've got to.

"I'm fine!" Emma shot into the restroom and planted herself in front of the sink and did just that, splashing water over her face. The cold confirmed she wasn't dreaming but did nothing to combat the aching fear running through her chest. Her heart pounded, beating with the adrenaline of the morning. She almost screamed when the door popped open behind her.

"Emma? What's…?" Mia grabbed some paper towels from the dispenser and handed them to her.

"I'm fine, really." Emma took the paper towels with a "thank you" and patted her face dry. Trying to be casual, knowing she was failing, she pulled her lip gloss from her pocket and reapplied it. She looked almost normal, if the mirror could be trusted. "But, hey, while you're here..."

Emma pushed a smile to her lips as she leaned against the sink. Her mind raced, looking for some way to bring up Ned without seeming insane.

Mia only stared, one eyebrow up near her hairline. "Yeah?"

"I've been meaning to ask about your brother. Something Keaton said in Richmond got me thinking about siblings, you know?" Emma worked up a casual laugh that sounded more like a crow's screech. She soldiered on, even as Mia's eyes widened. "What did he do? What was he like?"

"Uh, my brother? You want to know about Ned?"

"Yeah...unless you're in a hurry?" Emma forced a light-hearted grin and sipped her coffee.

Just two gals...having coffee in a public restroom...talking about deceased relatives...

Man, she was acting manic, but what choice did she have? If Ned was here, wanting something, the only thing Emma could do was try to get ahead of things before he really popped up at the wrong moment.

"Well...Ned was great. His job was boring compared to ours. He worked for a tech start-up. He was the right-hand man of the CEO or something. But he was...I mean...you know, he was my best friend."

Mia paused, as if waiting for something, but Emma kept her expression as neutral as possible. "I know he was. What was he like? Before the accident, I mean."

You dumbass. Of course you're asking about him before the accident.

Mia went to the sink and washed her hands, as if

searching for something to do. "He was a good guy. I don't know what you want me to say? We'd go to football games together." Mia dried her hands with a paper towel. "He always looked out for me and my parents, and he was smart. Really smart. He could've been the CEO of that company instead of the CEO's go-to guy. Why are you asking?"

"And he died in a car accident? Am I remembering that right? I'm wondering, just...was he upset about anything when he died? Something at work, maybe—"

Mia took a fast step toward her, cutting off Emma's stream of questions. She gripped Emma's hands. "What are you not telling me? What the heck is going on with you?"

Emma opened her mouth, looking for a believable lie, but couldn't find one. She gaped like a fish.

She wasn't approaching this well. Ned's ghost had thrown her, driving her to ask weirdly timed questions that were none of her business. Opening up old wounds on a Monday morning for no reason she could rightly explain.

Mia seemed to sense Emma's internal struggle and didn't push further. "Look, I'm here when you need me." Mia released her grip and backed off. "If you need something, tell me, okay? But make sure you get some sleep tonight. You look tired."

She could tell I was about to lie to her. Dammit.

Emma swallowed down the bitterness in her throat. She barely held herself back from asking Mia to stay behind and talk to her now. But there was no point.

Ghosts were trying to ruin her life, and the best Emma could do would be to avoid allowing them the pleasure.

She picked up her coffee and opened the restroom door, sweeping through with a confidence she didn't feel.

Emma did her best not to make eye contact with Ned's headless ghost, his features almost visible amid a cloud of what looked like blood or splattered brains. Emma couldn't guess, and didn't want to, so she veered and left him standing in the hallway as she made her way back to her desk.

6

If Emma had ever felt like a bigger horse's ass, she couldn't remember when.

Mia focused a little bit too hard on her doughnut and coffee, evading Emma's gaze as Emma sank into her desk chair and brought her cup of lukewarm coffee to her lips. She wanted some information on why Ned Logan might be so hell-bent on sticking around, but she'd pushed too hard. Whether or not he had unfinished business, Ned remained a mystery.

The only thing Emma had succeeded in doing was making Mia incredibly uncomfortable.

Leo leaned toward her from the next desk, narrow-eyed like he might be about to press her. Emma realized he—everyone—must've seen her hightail it to the bathroom.

A hearty knock from across the room saved her from her own awkwardness.

SSA Jacinda Hollingsworth stood in the doorway to her office at the edge of the bullpen, waving a folder in the air. She gestured them into the neighboring conference room. "Let's go, gang."

Saved by the caseload.

Emma was first into the conference room, grabbing the seat closest to Jacinda at the head of the table. Ned still roamed out in the bullpen, but the conference room was blessedly empty. Opening her iPad to take notes, Emma already had her eyes on the projector screen, feeling like an overeager student.

Jacinda hit the power button. "I hope you all weren't tired of the horror movie vibe after Little Clementine, because we've got another one for the books. You might not want to take any snacks along to these crime scenes."

Denae scoffed from across the table. "Don't tell me we've got vampires and werewolves to go with the Little Clementine axe murderer."

"No, but we do have grave robbers." Jacinda sighed and sat down at the head of the table, rubbing her forehead, and scowling over an open case file.

Emma waited for the punchline, but none came. "Are you serious, Jacinda? Grave robbing?"

Vance muttered a curse.

Jacinda swallowed hard, pressed a button, and lit up the screen at the front of the conference room.

It was difficult to parse what Emma saw. Gray dust had settled over the scene. She slowly realized the dust was from a pulverized stone crypt.

"Crypt robbing, to be specific," Jacinda continued. She pointed out the broken crypt, the hole where someone very determined had pulled the casket out. The casket lay on the floor with its upper half hacked to bits. "Detective Stanley Danielson has asked for our help with a crypt robber who's struck two different mausoleums on the last two consecutive nights. One in inner-city D.C. at Van Der Beek Cemetery, which you see here. A security service guard was making the rounds and reported a busted mausoleum door. The other incident was in a very old rural graveyard in Maryland. That one's the Angel Willows Cemetery. So the perpetrator is crossing jurisdictions."

As Jacinda took a sip of water, Leo broke in. "Any sign of how the bodies were moved? It's not like you can slip a dead body into your pocket."

Jacinda pulled her long red hair into a messy bun. Whenever her hair went up, the team was quickly learning, the situation was serious. "I didn't just reference the Little Clementine case for fun. Remember how the victims there were beheaded? Well…"

Mia let out a deep breath. "No. You can't be serious."

"I wish I weren't." Jacinda sighed, rubbing her forehead again. "The most troubling aspect of our new case is that our unsub disinterred only the heads. Then the sick fuck replaced them with the very fresh heads of other murdered men."

The screen shifted to a close-up of the hole in the coffin. A man's head lolled to the side, disconnected from the body below it.

Emma let out a disbelieving laugh because it was better than crying. Decapitated victims were following her around today. First Ned, now this. She tried to keep the mood light so her colleagues wouldn't sense her stress. "Grave robbing *and* dismemberment. Talk about a Monday for the books."

Meanwhile, Jacinda was already up at the whiteboard, writing details as she spoke. "The first, um, fresh head, for lack of a better term, has been identified as Jay South, manager of Scotch on Water. That's a D.C. bar with a fairly low-key reputation as dive bars go. South was thirty-seven years old. We do not have a murder scene, only the dumping scene, and only a partial at that."

Leo coughed. "I'm sorry, partial? How do we have a partial dumping scene?"

"His body is MIA, but Jay South's head was recovered from where it had been placed on the body of Sid Waller at Angel Willows Cemetery."

The SSA tapped on her iPad, and a nearly identical scene appeared on the screen—a broken crypt and a hacked-up coffin lid. Inside was Jay South's head staring straight up at the camera. Inches of blank space separated his head from the suit collar attached to Sid Waller's body.

At least there wasn't blood. These men had all been killed elsewhere, leading to a fairly clean crime scene.

Little Clementine's scenes hadn't been so tidy. Emma still remembered blood soaking through beds, floors, and saturating the dirt.

"Sid Waller's head is MIA," Jacinda continued. "Next, we have Terry Derby, a D.C. construction worker who was fifty years old. Local PD confirmed Mr. Derby was healthy as of a few days ago. His head was placed on the body of Marcus Peabody at Van Der Beek Cemetery." She switched the on-screen photo back to the first head.

Emma stared at the names on the board, separated into columns and figures already, only two days into a case. "I don't…I don't even know how to count victims on something like this. Two? Four?"

Jacinda sighed, her body seeming to deflate. She did not seem like herself.

From the look on his face, Leo seemed to be thinking the same thing.

He stood from the table and approached Jacinda at the board, speaking in a whisper. Jacinda began to shake her head, but then shrugged. The SSA sat at the table, leaving Leo at the board in her place.

"I don't feel great. I think I might've caught a bug." She waved Emma farther down the table.

Emma scooted down. "Oh no."

"You folks keep your distance." Her face was, indeed, pale. "Meanwhile, back to the case. To clarify, we have four victims, even though two of them didn't feel a thing. Authorities have no idea where the bodies of our newly dead victims are, nor where the stolen heads have been taken. As for the *why* of all this…your guess is as good as mine."

Vance pointed to the crypt column. "Any security footage?"

Jacinda shook her head. "There's no security coverage at Angel Willows Cemetery at all. The place is rural, not a lot of money for upkeep. The nearest surrounding CCTV camera footage is being recovered. We might be able to narrow down a list of vehicles from the nearby gas station footage. The nearest roads are seldom used, from what I understand. Van Der Beek Cemetery had one hidden external security cam hanging above the mausoleum doorframe. They apparently didn't see it, because there was no effort to cover the lens or stay outside line of sight. Our unsub damaged the door when they broke in. Looks like they used a sledgehammer."

Denae eyed the notes Leo continued writing up on the board. "Not exactly any finesse to that."

"Right. But we can rule out an inside job because they're smashing their way in. Plus, we have two crime scenes." Emma flicked through the file notes on her iPad. "How far apart are they? I doubt a worker would commute between them."

"That's a little something." Jacinda got up and placed sticky arrows on a map hanging at the side of the room, pointing out each cemetery's location, one in D.C. and the other across the Maryland state line. "They're not particularly close to each other, either, but they are out of the way. At the Van Der Beek Cemetery, Detective Danielson's officers examined the exterior security footage. They noted a person dressed entirely in black with a black ski mask covering their face. The perpetrator carried a black duffel bag, which the PD presumes held tools. The suspect's sex is undetermined, but we'll have the footage soon and can make our own observations."

"And this one person broke into the crypts?" Leo ran a hand through his curls, leaning back against the whiteboard. "That would take strength, right? Determination?"

"A lot of it." Emma leaned forward, eyeing the map. "And the removal and replacement of the heads…this sounds ritualistic, right? Like there's some kind of freaky plan in place that we're not seeing?"

"Are the victims connected?" Mia asked. "Any of them?"

"Not that we can tell so far." Jacinda flipped through the file in front of her and described their four victims.

No obvious connections surfaced between the four men, or even between any combination of two of them.

Mundane details like the men's ages, occupations, and marital statuses passed in and out of Emma's mind as quickly as the air through her lungs. It was already a monster of a case, and she was mentally exhausted by Ned's ceaseless appearances that morning. And who knew what was coming?

More headless ghosts. *As if I haven't seen enough.*

Maybe another appointment with Marigold would help her clarify things and…prepare? When she'd woken that morning, she'd been optimistic. Ned had sucked that optimism right out of her.

Focus on the case, Emma girl.

It was time to get to work, ghosts or no ghosts.

7

Leo chanced a quick glance sideways. Denae propped her hand companionably against the side of Leo's seat, her wrist close enough that he could just smell her perfume. She looked good. Like she belonged beside him.

Though she'd probably look better in his truck on the way to a movie rather than in the fleet Explorer going to a morgue.

Denae cleared her throat, directing him back to business, as if she could hear him. She pointed to the upcoming turn for the M.E.'s office.

He wouldn't have put it past her to know his thoughts already. The woman was smart and well out of his league. Though he wouldn't tell her so.

"You know the M.E. well?" He slowed for the turn, seeing the first sign for the building ahead.

"We've met. Dr. Bryan knows what she's doing...been here going on a decade now, if I remember right. Once we get inside, you'll want to go around to the right of the building to get to the parking garage. First level has an entrance we can access through security with our badges and go straight in."

Leo processed the directions as they came. He was happy to be around Denae once again, but now they were back to work after the weekend's dates, he was also a little tongue-tied. The smallest interactions carried an awkward note. Based on her easy manner, he couldn't say she felt the same. He, on the other hand, had almost dropped his coffee when she'd smiled at him in the break room that morning.

Denae typed something into her phone, answering a text from Jacinda. "She's stuck in traffic, and it looks like Emma is too. We might be out of here before they get to Van Der Beek."

Leo turned into the parking garage. "Speaking of Emma, you talk to her this morning? She seemed spastic as hell."

"Eh, that's just Emma. She has her cray-cray days, but she's a pro. You'll get used to it."

"I don't know…you're not concerned?" Leo focused on the Explorer as he navigated the garage. He hated maneuvering through tight, dark parking areas. "Didn't seem like she could focus on a conversation for more than two seconds."

"Huh, was she that bad?" Denae frowned for a second, pointing him toward a ramp leading to a lower level. "I guess I must've been distracted. How dare you."

"What? I…" Leo blinked, slowing the vehicle. Denae laughed in response, and he couldn't help grinning back at her. "I distracted *you*, you mean."

She chuckled, prodding his shoulder with her fist. "You were a lot smoother before we started flirting with each other, Agent Ambrose. Something's a little backward about that."

You got that right.

"You're good at knocking a guy off his game, Agent Monroe, there's no denying it."

He found a parking spot far away from the lower entrance as they also moved far away from the subject of Emma Last. Which was fine. It wasn't like he had much more to say on the matter. Emma had seemed so off that morning, he'd been concerned.

Denae led the way to a security gate at the far rear of the garage's first level, flashing her badge to the bored guard on duty.

Inside, the bright hallway with its polished floors reminded Leo of state-of-the-art hospitals. The windows into offices were so shiny they were like mirrors. The tiles were so clean they were almost slippery. But the air was stale and too antiseptic to be comfortably breathable.

Ahead of him, Denae was already greeting a middle-aged blond woman in a white coat. She waved him forward and offered a smile that seemed a shade too bright for a Monday morning and somehow matched the floors. "You must be Agent Ambrose. I'm Dr. Mary Bryan. Call me Mary."

"Nice to meet you, Mary." Leo shook her hand and took the mask she offered as Denae donned a similar one.

"For the smell." She opened the door to the morgue, ushering them inside. "Though I don't know what good it'll do. Ventilation's gone wonky again."

You could say that again.

A sour smell of death meshed with the tang of chemicals. The scent made Leo's nose itch, but at least grounded him in the moment.

The first two metal tables were occupied with the identified bodies so far. Mary had stripped the men of their death clothes to examine their new, postmortem wounds closer. Strange odors floated from the headless corpses, but it wasn't decay, since they'd been dead awhile. A sticky note had been set on each table, identifying the bodies for the short term.

Marcus Peabody smelled dusty more than anything. Sid Waller smelled like he'd been buried in some chemical cologne.

Denae moved forward to a third table with two telltale lumps pushing up white sheets.

The heads.

"What do you know?"

Mary moved up beside Denae and, without fanfare, pulled back the cloth to show the propped-up heads of Jay South and Terry Derby, both slack-jawed and leaning against little foam pads, triangle-shaped and absurdly white.

"I think a saw was used to remove both heads. See the rough edges?" She pointed along the skin of the necks, which was puckered and torn. "No signs of struggle, like bludgeoning, but that's not saying much. There was a distinct lack of blood at the dumping scenes. Means they were killed elsewhere and were possibly dead before they were decapitated and placed with…"

"New bodies." Denae leaned forward, bringing herself face-to-face with the first victim, Jay South. "White, blond, and blue-eyed."

"And he looks fairly fit…his cheeks aren't very chubby anyway." Leo glanced from one head to the other. "So does Terry Derby, if a little older. His background says he was a construction worker, so that makes sense."

"Both their eyes were closed." Mary used a pointer to indicate the closed eyes, which were sunken in their sockets. "I swabbed the skin for foreign DNA. Sent that off. We'll have toxicology reports in a few weeks, too, but until then, unless you bring me their bodies, it's going to be pretty impossible to make any educated guesses as to how they were killed."

Leo leaned in closer as Mary angled up the heads, showing where the saw cut through the men's bones and muscles postmortem. Disturbing as the sight was, Leo was more bothered by the sour-sweet scent of decay and chemicals.

Even though the solitary heads pointed to obvious violence, they weren't near the worst thing Leo had seen, even in the last month. From Denae's easy stance beside him, he guessed she'd have said the same.

"I know I'm not giving you much to work with." Mary pulled off her gloves and tossed them in a nearby trash can. "Beyond the obvious, what I've got is pretty cut-and-dried so far. The detective asked me to make note of any similarities between the victims, but I've got nothing. They're not even the same blood type. Just two middle-aged white men, one with blond hair and one with brown."

Leo followed the doctor toward the door, not bothering to linger. Visiting the bodies—for what they were—was a matter of course, but they hadn't expected to learn much of anything there. "Let us know if you get anything else."

Mary raised an eyebrow. "Like their actual bodies? I think that's your department, Agent Ambrose."

Touché.

8

Mia hummed to herself. She was only half-focused on their surroundings as Vance maneuvered them through traffic on the way to question Terry Derby's ex-wife.

Despite the gruesome nature of their case, the day seemed bright. Optimistic. After a whole weekend spent with Vance, she noted transitioning into a Monday morning together felt so incredibly easy, it was unreal.

Didn't expect to feel this way anytime soon. But...it's nice to know my heart still works.

Mia rested her hand against Vance's forearm, stretching over the divider between the SUV's front seats. A warm thrum of affection buzzed through her, heightening her nerves when he smiled at her. It'd been a long time since she'd felt so connected, so in sync with someone else.

"I'm glad you transferred up here. It's funny, us being so... happy together. Already." Vance broke off, his soft voice barely audible over the radio.

She kept her response light, not wanting to get too emotional before interviewing bereaved family members. "You mean we're not supposed to be in a good mood while investigating beheadings and crypt robberies? Just because we're part of the FBI's Violent Crimes Unit doesn't mean we can't have fun."

"And an odd morning doesn't mean we're not in for a great week." Vance gripped her hand. "I'm glad you're shaking it off. I like hearing you hum along with the radio."

Mia worked to keep the smile on her face, taking some comfort from his presence. What an odd morning they'd had.

And her mind kept going back to Emma's bizarre behavior.

Weird even for Emma.

Was it possible the Little Clementine murders had taken more of a toll on the agent than she'd been willing to admit?

Emma had witnessed a grief-stricken woman shove a vile man to his death from a cliff top. That couldn't have been easy.

Or maybe something had happened when Emma had gone to visit Keaton over the weekend? They'd always claimed to be best friends, but maybe there was more between them...and something had gone wrong?

No, that didn't seem like the right conclusion, either way.

Keaton had nothing to do with her brother. And Ned was the center of the morning's strangeness. *What was up with all the questions about my brother?*

When Vance finally pulled into the driveway of the Arts and Crafts bungalow, parking behind a jacked-up pickup truck and a little sports car, he turned and booped her on the nose. "Worries off."

She made a show of nipping at his finger. "You wish you could turn me off."

"Actually...no." His eyes remained tight on hers until a blush warmed her cheeks.

"You're such a flirt." Mia grabbed her bag from the floorboard and ignored her partner's gaze, as well as the little flutter in her belly. This was not the time.

And as if to highlight that fact, the door of the little D.C. home was already opening...framing a shirtless man who looked none too pleased at their presence. The man's muscles were flexed, and he filled most of the doorway.

Mia came around the front of the SUV to meet Vance and put up a united front. "He look strong enough to break crypts and haul coffins?"

"Definitely."

Together, they started toward the front porch with every one of Mia's Spidey-senses tingling.

The pavers beneath her feet disappeared fast, and beside her, Vance shifted his coat open to show his gun. They hadn't expected to greet a threat alongside the ex-wife of the latest victim.

Mia was just about to speak when a smaller woman shoved herself in front of the man, turning her head to say something over her shoulder. Whatever had been said, it was too soft for Mia to hear, but the man stepped back reluctantly.

As Mia and Vance approached, the walking pile of sinew still blocked entry to the house, his bulging muscles remaining fully flexed. The sight would have been comical if not for the implied threat.

"I'm Janet Schmidt. Please don't mind my husband, Jack." She tilted her head to indicate Mr. Musclehead. "You must be the agents in charge of investigating my ex-husband's murder?" The brunette held the screen door wide open, a tight smile on her face. "I don't know how we can help, but I'm glad you're here. We've all been on edge."

The bodybuilder grunted and retreated into the house, out of sight. Since Janet was ignoring him, Mia did as well. "I'm Special Agent Mia Logan, and this is my partner, Special

Agent Vance Jessup. Thanks for taking time out to meet with us."

Stepping past Janet, Mia found herself in an open-concept living room. Shirtless Jack stood off to the side, a scowl on his face. Two red-faced teenagers sat on one side of a large sectional sofa that took up much of the living area. Terry Derby's kids, presumably.

"I doubt we can tell you anything we haven't already told the cops." Jack stepped forward, focused on Vance. "Can we make this quick? Janet's gotta plan her ex-husband's funeral since his family isn't worth shit. We didn't plan on the guy taking over our week."

Janet slapped him on the arm, giving him a stare.

The brown-eyed girl on the couch dropped her head into her hands.

This guy is a douche and a half.

Mia focused on Janet rather than her new husband. "We won't take up more time than we have to, Mrs. Schmidt. Why don't we all just take a seat?"

As if all she needed was permission, Janet collapsed onto the couch.

Vance shifted to the oversize ottoman to be more parallel with the grieving ex-wife, and Mia sat beside him.

Mr. Shirtless-and-Insensitive went around the couch and stood behind Janet with his arms crossed, looming over them.

Mia worked to ignore him, fearing she might release all the pent-up laughter the man had so far inspired. How long could he keep his chest and arms flexed like that anyway?

As if hearing her silent question, the idiot flexed his pecs to make his chest muscles dance. The teenage boy scoffed, and she liked him all the more for it.

"Mrs. Schmidt, I'm sorry for your loss." Vance leaned

forward to speak directly to the teens. "For all your losses. Maybe we could start by hearing when you last saw Terry?"

Janet reached a hand across her chest, and to Mia's great surprise, the ox she'd married deigned to lower one arm and take his wife's hand where it rested on her shoulder. He didn't step forward, though, leaving a few inches of space between them. She clung to his fingers as she answered. "Terry picked up the kids…Lindsey and Aaron…" She looked at the teens and went quiet, as if she'd nothing left to say.

Mia cleared her throat. "Mrs. Schmidt, you were telling us about the last time you saw Terry."

The woman startled and shifted to meet Mia's eyes again. "Of course. It was last Sunday. Here. He came by, like he always did. They spend…spent…most of their time with Terry at his house. It's nearer to their school."

Lindsay shot a silent, distasteful glance at her stepfather. Mia had a pretty solid sense that proximity to school wasn't the only reason these kids had preferred their dad's house.

These poor kids. They have nowhere else to go now.

"And did he say anything out of the ordinary when he picked them up?" Vance asked.

"No…I'm sorry. He seemed normal. Maybe even… happier than he had lately. Chipper. But he loves…dammit, *loved*…our kids more than anything. He was always happy to be with them."

Mia leaned forward and settled one hand on the woman's knee. "I understand this is hard. Maybe let's back up. Was Terry okay with the divorce? Was he starting a new life, like you are?"

"What the hell are you implying, lady?" Mr. Shirtless-and-Stupid crowded up to the couch directly behind his wife.

"Jack!" Janet grew a bit of backbone and glared up at him. "Let them do their jobs. Why don't you go work on lunch for the kids?"

For a second, Mia thought he would refuse, but after another arm flex, Jack the Lifter turned and stalked away. She wondered if he hated Terry enough to kill him.

Maybe. But to cut off his head and stick it on another dead body? That took dedication, and a degree of malevolence or delusion that I'm not seeing from Mr. Flex here. At least, not yet.

Janet's unfocused gaze remained on Jack for another few seconds as he walked away, then she turned her pale face back to the agents. "Ignore him. Terry's a sore subject, since the kids never really…uh…" She glanced at her children. "Took to Jack."

"We understand." Vance's remark was flat, but Mia heard the irony.

"The divorce wasn't exactly mutual, but it wasn't ugly." Janet shifted, lowering her voice after glancing again toward her kids, who kept their faces carefully neutral. Their expressions seemed to be long practiced. "And it was the right thing for everyone. I left Terry about a year ago, and I admit the remarriage was fast." The woman straightened her sweater, speaking quietly enough that Mia barely heard her. "But you have to understand Jack and I hit it off immediately, and we…uh…knew each other before Terry and I separated."

"Mom's a stereotype." Aaron Derby, the older teen, cut in, his anger clear. "The suburban housewife who ran off with her personal trainer."

Lindsay smacked him on the arm, hard. The younger teen seemed to have assumed a peacekeeper position.

Janet only grimaced. "My son's right. I am a stereotype. Being a decade older than Jack doesn't help the picture, but it is what it is. Terry was good about it, though…he was a good man."

"You hurt him." Aaron wasn't ready to let his mother off the hook. Mia predicted there would be several rough months ahead for this family.

"We'd just grown apart." Janet didn't look at her son—though the next words were about him and his sister. "And the kids are old enough to understand the way of things. There was no reason to stay together on their behalf any longer. Lindsay's fifteen and Aaron's seventeen...they've been through a lot." She curled in on herself, shaking her head.

Terry's ex-wife was close to breaking down right in front of them. Understandable, after having to identify her husband's head at the morgue that morning.

But there was something off, selfish maybe, about the woman.

Mia shifted sideways, focusing on the teens. "And you two were the ones who realized your dad was missing? Do I have that right, Lindsay? Aaron?"

Lindsay's brown eyes were red rimmed from crying. "Dad didn't come home when he said he would. He said he was just going out for dinner and would be back before Aaron and I went to bed. He should've been home by nine. Nine thirty at the latest."

Jack returned to the living room and leaned against the doorframe.

Mia ignored him. "And did he go out for dinner often when you kids were at the house?"

"He almost never went out, and we were almost always there." A sadness, which seemed old, crossed Aaron's face. "Dad's life was work and us. We kept telling him he should go out with friends, see someone...and he looked nice yesterday. Dressed up. Even washed his truck after the snow melted."

"I think he was going on a date." Lindsay choked back a sob, the tragedy of the idea seeming to strike her physically.

A bark of a laugh cut into the room. "Old-timer finally found his rebound broad."

Both teenagers glared at their stepfather. Aaron's fists clenched, and Mia prepared herself to jump between the two.

But it was Janet who jumped in instead. "Shut up, Jack. Now is not the time."

Mia's eyebrows shot up. She hadn't expected Janet to have that kind of force in her. Yet Jack shut up.

Aaron's fists clenched.

"He didn't say where he was going? Didn't leave a phone number?" Mia directed her questions at Lindsay, letting Aaron glare things out with his stepfather. "Mention a particular restaurant or highway he'd be traveling, maybe?"

Lindsay shook her head as tears leaked down her cheeks. The teenager didn't even seem to notice she was crying. Sadness had enveloped her, seeming to become a part of her. Mia's heart broke.

Vance sighed, flipping the cover closed on his iPad. "Mrs. Schmidt, the problem we're having is that we have no idea where Terry went after leaving his house. Law enforcement determined his phone was with him. The last tower ping indicates he was in the northern D.C. suburbs after leaving home that evening, but then nothing. It's possible he drove into a dead zone or his phone was destroyed. But until the police are able to pull his phone records, the best we can do is ask questions and wait for the CCTV footage to be pulled from homes and businesses surrounding his house. And that takes time."

"Which is why *anything you can tell us* could be helpful." Mia clasped her hands on her lap. "Did he have any enemies? Could someone have set him up? Maybe he owed money or had a tiff with a business colleague or former customer?"

"Dad didn't fight with anyone." Aaron leapt to his feet and paced across the room. He stared out the front window, back turned to the agents. For a moment, Mia thought he might be lying, but then she saw his shoulders shudder. The seventeen-year-old just didn't want them to see him crying. He couldn't quite hide the tremble in his voice as he continued. "Everyone liked him. You should see all the stuff he did with Habitat for Humanity. Guys like that don't have enemies."

"Dad loved everyone, and everyone loved him." Lindsay agreed. "He didn't just act like a people person. He *was* a people person."

Janet moved to her daughter's side and wrapped her arms around her as the girl began sobbing outright. "The kids are right. I wish we could help you, but my ex-husband was the kindest man in the world. And the most responsible too. He didn't have enemies. If feathers ever got ruffled because he won a contract over some other firm, he smoothed them out. The man was a saint. Too good for me."

Mia glanced at Shirtless Jack, who sat on the couch, taking his wife's vacated spot. He scowled at her words but didn't argue the point.

Vance pulled business cards out of his pocket and left them on the coffee table.

Mia picked up a card and crouched in front of Janet and Lindsay. She lowered her voice, hoping Shirtless Jack wouldn't overhear. "If you think of anything else, any of you, please call. And I promise we'll be in touch as soon as we know more."

Translation? We'll call you when we find the body.

9

A windblown arrangement of frayed fabric flowers littered the walkway. Emma stepped over them, and Jacinda followed. The lost decoration was emblematic of Van Der Beek Cemetery. Once, the graveyard was well-manicured with highly sought-after plots, but now, it was mostly old graves of the lost and forgotten.

Pulling her coat tighter, she led Jacinda toward what remained of Marcus Peabody's crypt and casket. Ahead of them, a smog-stained stone mausoleum bustled with forensic techs coming and going. A plainclothes detective stood outside, smoking.

"Detective Stanley Danielson?" Jacinda stood back and waved to the detective, who Emma had met a few times before. "We spoke on the phone. I'm SSA Jacinda Hollingsworth, and I believe you've met Special Agent Last?"

Danielson greeted them as he stubbed out his cigarette. "My pleasure, once again. Glad to have you."

Emma had met Danielson a couple of years ago during a training session on behavioral analysis. They were both the type to talk too much in the back of the room and had been called out more than once during that weekend. She remembered Danielson as professional but supremely uninterested in performing role-playing tasks. Though, she recalled, he'd made a pretty convincing bank robber.

Ushering them into the mausoleum, he pointed to an emptied crypt halfway down the wall, on the second tier up, about waist height. A gaping casket sat nearby, with a ragged hole in its lid.

A young tech walked out of the entrance, shaking his head at Danielson as they passed each other. The surrounding techs inside collected evidence that appeared to be made up of splinters.

Inside, the mausoleum was in only slightly better shape than the cemetery at large, assuming Emma ignored the hacked-up casket and broken crypt. A dingy light illuminated the worst of the shadows. The air smelled of dust and winter.

And there are no ghosts here. Just like in this whole damn cemetery so far. What gives?

"Anything yet?" Jacinda asked.

"Not much, aside from the obvious. No fingerprints or blood, so there's no chance this was our murder scene, like I told you on the phone. Only thing recovered so far is a single, long brown hair. Might be our unsub's, might not. Impossible to tell when the strand was left here."

Emma glanced around the space. "And this is a community mausoleum? Open to the public?"

A tech thrust a clipboard at Danielson to sign. "Yeah, and the place gets its fair share of visitors. Especially to the crypts. They're the nicest part of the cemetery. Somebody spent real money to have our Mr. Peabody interred."

"With his original head."

Emma's mutter brought a tilt to the detective's lips. "Right. And now that's gone, along with the family's peace of mind. Still…who knows? Maybe that hair we found will tell us something. It's bagged and sent to the lab for analysis, just in case."

"Could give us the racial group. DNA, if the root's intact." Jacinda pointed at the casket. "You already removed Mr. Peabody's remains. Anything else of note?"

"*Nada*. No witnesses either. Not yet anyway."

Emma stepped over to the mausoleum's entrance and peeked outside. Even though the time was approaching noon, not a single visitor wandered among the headstones. No car parked on the lanes weaving back and forth through the cemetery. "We're pretty deep into the roughest part of D.C. Guessing witnesses won't be leaping to talk to the cops or the Feds."

"Right." Danielson sighed and stepped outside before pulling out another cigarette. Emma followed him, staying a few paces back as he lit up.

Danielson blew out a cloud of smoke and looked back to the mausoleum. "We've only got external footage of the suspect entering and leaving with a bag of tools. Hell, even if someone saw our guy, it's unlikely they approached him. Not in this area. People here mind their own business, and to be honest, just walking around here at night is pretty ill-advised."

Emma couldn't disagree. Come sundown, she wouldn't be caught walking alone in this area without her gun and badge at the ready. "Guessing you've got officers canvassing the neighborhood anyway, just in case?"

"Par for the course." Danielson nodded. "And I'll let you know if they come back with anything. If you two don't need anything else, though..." He waggled his cigarette and headed off to stand among the headstones.

Emma grinned. "Enjoy the cold, Stanley."

She rejoined Jacinda inside, and they made a fast circuit of the building's inner landscape. Covering their noses to ward off the musty odor, Emma and Jacinda peered into the barren crypt, which Marcus Peabody had occupied for six years, but Emma saw nothing of note.

Back outside, she led the way down the path toward the Explorer, keeping her eyes peeled for ghosts. Although she'd seen her share of the dead over the course of the last twenty-four hours, the cemetery was deserted. Quiet and empty of any persons but living law enforcement.

She'd just about given up on seeing even one spirit when a diminutive shape caught her eye, nearly causing her to trip on her own feet.

Midway through the cemetery, drifting along on a collision course with the path Emma and Jacinda followed, a ghost finally made an appearance.

Dressed in a blue Easter dress and bonnet five decades out of fashion was a young girl with a giant hole through her chest, attesting to her violent cause of death. She drifted along, even though Emma could clearly see the girl taking steps. She seemed aimless, as if she'd found the path and decided to take a stroll.

Emma tried not to stare at the spirit as she approached. She stretched her steps to move farther ahead of her supervisor. If she could put some distance between herself and Jacinda, maybe she could have a conversation with this spirit and learn something about the case...without any insensible dialogue making Emma seem like she was ripe for the nut farm.

A dozen strides away from the ghost, Emma chanced a whispered, "Hi."

She hoped the word sounded like a casual huff of breath in the cold. The last thing Emma needed was Jacinda catching her talking to the air.

The dead girl—maybe eight years old?—jerked straight,

stepping off the path she'd been walking, and looked up at Emma with wide white eyes and a gaping mouth.

A moment later, she was gone.

So much for that idea.

Emma bit back a sigh and stopped on the path, waiting for Jacinda to catch up. Her heart pounded with annoyance. The irony in the air was thick enough to swim through. Why, when she wanted to speak to a ghost, did they refuse to speak to her? Ghosts could surround her at her workplace or apartment, but not at a fucking cemetery?

The urge to scream was just as strong as the urge to laugh.

Whether the ghosts were trying to drive her insane was a moot point.

They were doing a damn good job of it either way.

10

"Spirit, soul, body. Spirit, soul, body. Spirit, soul, body."

My chant hung in the air as I tipped the wheelbarrow forward.

Our special delivery rolled over the edge of the pier and into the ice-cold lake before us.

Terry Derby's corpse was unrecognizable as it sank, wrapped inside a tarp, weighted down with junk auto parts, and duct-taped like crazy. I knew from years of swimming in this lake that there was a steep drop-off before this point of the pier.

The lake had barely frozen this year, so the body shattered the thin surface ice like glass.

The sound was satisfying.

As he sank, bubbles drifted upward as whatever air was left in Terry's body burst through the surface. Then the surge stopped, almost as suddenly as it had begun.

Terry's corpse would reach the bottom in short order.

Pulling the empty wheelbarrow across the wooden boards, I stepped off the pier and glanced over at Michael. He stood on a little promontory overlooking the still water.

With his arms crossed, a confident smile on his face, and his blue eyes shining in the sunlight filtering down through our wooded land, he appeared satisfied.

I brought the wheelbarrow to a stop beside him. "I still don't know what to do about the heads."

He didn't answer, but he'd frowned when I placed Mr. Peabody's head, bound in plastic wrap, into our storage freezer in the lake house basement. He was right. A freezer wasn't a fitting resting place for the heads of men who'd, by all accounts, been decent. Not even temporarily.

I'd been careful to search everything I could find on the men I would kill and the men whose corpses I would transform. It hadn't been easy, digging through pages and pages of newspaper archives online. Obituary after obituary.

I almost gave up more than once, feeling the challenge too much. All that information, all those names, and the stories of the lives the men had lived. So many of them reminded me of my Michael. In the end, that was what kept me going. Knowing I would be choosing the right vessels to complete my ritual.

Still, I couldn't stop thinking about the wives and children who were left behind when the men took their last breaths. And that got me thinking about the people left to mourn the men I had killed, and those I would kill over the next two days.

"Maybe we should return them to the families?"

Michael leaned back against a tree, a scowl hardening his features. I knew that expression…it meant he thought my idea might endanger the plan. Which made sense.

A nice idea, but hard to pull off without getting in trouble. And we had to focus on the restoration.

I peeled off my work gloves and rubbed my hands together. The gloves stank of embalming chemicals and bodily decay but made the work just a bit easier on my senses.

Not a single blister yet, even after all that work last night, but they might be on the way.

No matter. Progress was being made. My husband and I would have our future together, regardless of how that damn car accident tried to steal him from me. I just had to stay focused.

Michael had been gone for three years. Now, we only had three days to work and focus to restore him before he drifted away into a world I couldn't reach.

"I wish I could touch you." I reached for him, but he stepped away, shaking his head.

My throat burned with emotion. He didn't like me reaching through him, and I supposed I didn't blame him. It was hard not to touch him, though. Not to at least try.

I forced my gaze back to the lake, to the dark watery spot where Terry Derby had disappeared beneath the surface. He'd been a nice man.

"Isn't it sad that not everyone knows the Force of Three? It's tragic how close they could keep their loved ones if only they took the right initiative. If only…"

Michael squinted into the distance, his lips parting as if in thought before he answered. Always so careful with his words. "Keep the information to yourself, Renata love. Omne trium perfectum."

Right. Our mantra to survive this process. To succeed in regaining the perfection we once shared. *Stick to the plan, stick to the ritual, and we will be whole again.*

Michael and I had enjoyed such a perfect marriage, a perfect union of bodies, minds, and spirits. Like my mother, he saw the value in spiritual connections, and believed in the Force of Three when I first explained it to him.

We'd been dating for three months, and he was my third

boyfriend. I knew it would be perfect with him, but I had to know how he would respond to the Force of Three. Even then, when I had known for over ten years that the Force of Three ruled everything in the universe, I still had to test Michael's acceptance. His willingness to see what I had always felt to be true.

And he had not disappointed in the slightest.

When I told him of the great design of the universe, how everything was centered around connections that came in threes, his eyes lit up with what I could only call recognition. He'd practically begged me to tell him more, to reveal all the wisdom and truth I had longed to share with a partner.

My previous relationships hadn't worked out because they had only been steps along the path. My first boyfriend was a fantastic lover but had no interest in joining me in conversations about anything beyond sex. And where he failed to stimulate my mind, my second relationship was with a man who could barely get me hot enough to melt butter.

They'd both failed but had served a purpose just the same. They prepared me to meet the man who would satisfy me in every way. Michael was my perfect mate physically, intellectually, and spiritually.

His cautious steps got my attention, and I turned to see him coming toward me. His raised eyebrows and his hand extended toward the water told me I'd missed something. But what? I'd contained Terry Derby's body so well, there was no chance bits of him might find their way to the surface, no matter how many fish managed to nibble their way to his flesh.

I looked to Michael for an explanation. He merely lifted a finger to his brow and tapped. Three times, of course.

"You want me to get rid of the heads in the lake?" My voice was a whisper, barely carrying, but he nodded.

Michael, as always, was right.

I turned to face the water again. Nobody would see anything. Nobody would be fishing or boating or combing the bottom for bodies. Nobody would catch us.

Anything I dropped below the dark surface—heads, torsos, *anything*—would sink down and be forgotten.

Michael loomed beside me, his voice barely competing with the lapping water. "Isn't the lake peaceful?"

Peaceful.

"Peace is all I want. With you." I entwined my fingers together, pretending it was Michael's firm grasp holding my hand, and closed my eyes. "You're...right. This is a perfect, peaceful resting place. And these men's sacrifices will keep you with me."

Here, at our lake, I could speak to Michael freely and nobody would think me crazy. I could stand here with my eyes closed and do what I had to do, and nobody would be the wiser. Nobody would know.

"You're my everything, Michael. I don't know what I'd do if I lost you forever."

The possibility sat heavy in the air. Before tears could really come, I straightened and turned back to my husband. "You're right. I'll put the heads to rest in the lake along with the bodies. I'm just tired...not thinking straight."

Michael's endearing snaggletooth winked white as the snow as he smiled in the sunlit afternoon. It nearly melted my heart. My man was right. I could do this. *We* could do this.

I finally turned and began tugging the wheelbarrow back up to the house, ignoring the ache in my back and my upper arms.

Terry's head certainly hadn't cut itself off. And after all that crypt work with the sledgehammer and hatchet, I could have curled up and slept for days.

Michael was unflappable, fit and trim and watchful.

I nearly tripped on the stone barrier running between the driveway and the path to the lake. Michael huffed behind me, whispering support.

"This is crunch time, Renata. Day two. Spirit, soul, body."

The heft of his words sat silent between us. I understood. I could sleep when the ritual was over.

"And then your life will be restored." My answer was automatic. Rote.

Spirit, soul, body…three days, and we were on day two. I could do this.

With the wheelbarrow stored beneath the porch—I'd need that contraption again soon enough, after all—I blew Michael a kiss and headed inside. The path of the sun told me it was time to think about dinner…I couldn't buy poisoned lasagna or wolfsbane at the grocery store, after all.

And in my opinion, Rick Royer deserved the best of both.

After our initial meeting on the internet and three months of incessant chatting, I knew what I needed to know. Rick Royer was an office supply store manager, a Gemini, and seemed very genuine, like my Michael.

Rick's weekend business trip was perfectly timed. Sure, I'd encouraged him to come this exact weekend, but the fact he'd agreed so easily was nothing less than serendipitous.

As I'd told Michael when Rick accepted my suggestion, it was fate.

I headed to the freezer and selected my third homemade lasagna, identical to the ones I'd served Terry Derby and Jay South. I'd made four in preparation for this process, one for the practice, and the all-important three for the ritual itself. Best to be prepared, and who wanted to cook in the middle of all the other chores I needed to accomplish?

As I lifted the aluminum foil-covered dish, I smiled

apologetically at Marcus Peabody's head beside it. "Sorry. I'll put you to rest soon."

I returned to the kitchen and set the lasagna on the counter.

I'd grown the magic ingredient myself in my little greenhouse. Wolfsbane was the heart of the plan. My patch of the plant flowered purple and gorgeous…ripe for plucking. And cooking.

I'd read that symptoms of exposure to wolfsbane could appear anywhere from twenty minutes to two hours after contact. But Michael and I agreed—vehemently—that I shouldn't let the victims linger for so long.

No, the faster I could get them dead, the faster I could get to the cemeteries and take care of business. And the less time I'd have to avoid them seeking help from anyone but me. That meant plenty of wolfsbane in each dish of lasagna, and my recipe was working just fine so far.

Sensing Michael looming over me as I pulled the aluminum foil off the dish, my exhausted muscles relaxed. His presence was comforting, letting me know I wasn't in this alone. "You watching me work, dear?"

He didn't answer, but that was fine. We agreed.

I made short work of getting the dish into the oven.

When that was done, I washed my hands and snarfed down a sandwich and drank sixteen ounces of water. There was no time for a nap, but it was important to stay nourished and hydrated if we were going to succeed.

Letting the lasagna cook, I wandered back toward the bedroom to pick out a crimson lipstick that would impress any date.

Michael had certainly liked it.

Makeup decided, I searched through my closet and chose a tight blue skirt I could wear over black leggings—easy to just drop the skirt before the real labor of the night—and a loose-fitting blouse that Michael had always loved.

I modeled the outfit for my husband when he appeared in the doorway, eyeing me with clear longing. And was that jealousy too? "Don't worry. This date is only for your benefit. All of this is fate."

Glancing back at my reflection, I couldn't help but grin.

My heart went positively light as a feather when I thought of Rick arriving in a few hours. Based on our online chats, his temperament reminded me so much of Michael's, which surely meant he was the perfect soul for this second day's work. Perfect for the ritual.

I turned and smiled at my husband. "Nearly time for date number two. Dinner's cooking, and then we'll go get that soul."

11

Leo pulled the fleet Explorer up to the front of Angel Willows Cemetery, coming to a stop just a few feet from the gate. The place was rural and deserted, so there was no need to parallel park.

The groundskeeper had promised to meet them at the entrance.

Denae slammed the passenger's side door and met him at the front of the wrought iron gate. "They closed the whole place?"

"They're probably being cautious. It's not easy explaining dismemberment to victims' loved ones, you know."

Leo waved at an approaching man beyond the gate. The man sped up a touch. His bald head gleamed in the afternoon sun. When he came closer, Leo stepped directly up to the gate and called out. "Ed Macintosh?"

The groundskeeper snorted in response as he yanked a key ring from the inside of his down coat. Sweat beaded on Ed's sunburned scalp, despite the chilly January afternoon. "What other fool'd be here to greet you?"

"Right." Leo waited for the man to open the gate and step back. "I hear we're lucky you found the crime scene so fast. Wanna tell us about it as you lead the way?"

The man emitted a sort of grumble from his throat before leading them directly over the grass and between headstones. He swiped at the sweat on his head with a red bandana. "*Lucky's* one way to put it. For you, not me. I coulda gone my whole damn life not seeing what I saw. This place is so out in the boonies, I'm only out here once a month or so for routine maintenance."

Denae tripped on a stray tree root.

Leo caught her elbow as she nearly went down, but the groundskeeper didn't slow. She shrugged and called ahead. "Mr. Macintosh, what led you to the crime scene? Did you see anyone coming or going?"

"Ha!" The man whirled, giving them time to catch up. The guy was scrawny, but fast as a weasel. "What kind of cemetery this look like to you? You see anyone banging on the gates to come in, even though we had the gates locked up all day?"

"Not exactly."

"Well, there ya go." The man turned back around, cutting across grass rather than sticking to any path. Far ahead, a stone mausoleum that had seen better days loomed out of some shrubbery. "I tend to a lot of rural graveyards, on a rotation, you understand, and I ain't seen a visitor to Angel Willows in the last year, at least. Even then, only on the weekends. Granted, I guess this happened on a weekend, but you can bet I was home asleep in the middle of the night. Nobody pays me enough to guard these places. I just take care of the grounds."

Leo sidestepped a large mud puddle and pushed aside branches from a weeping willow as they approached the mausoleum. Its door hung open, crooked on busted hinges. A flash of yellow crime scene tape could be seen just inside.

Macintosh came to a fumbling stop at the steps of the structure and leaned one hand against the rail. "I saw the door open is what happened. I was cutting back the branches over there." He gestured toward the weeping willow Leo had pushed through. "And I noticed this place standing open like this. Door ain't closed right after being broken into. People with relatives here have keys, or they call the cemetery office and arrange to be let in. Whoever bashed in these hinges did a fair bit of damage. And what kind of sick son of a gun messes with the dead anyway? Ain't that satanic?"

"Well, it's disrespectful at the very least. You mind waiting for us out here?"

The man nodded. "I got some gear, so I'll clip some of these bushes."

Leo stepped forward with Denae, letting the groundskeeper go.

He slipped on gloves before pressing open the door and stepping inside the dim mausoleum.

Crime scene tape hung across the doorway. The barrier was low enough that Leo could step over. Considering the number of cracked and half-buried headstones they'd passed, he was a little surprised the cemetery supported an above-ground mausoleum. Maybe the place had been more affluent at some time in the past.

"Place seems random, doesn't it?" Leo read the dates on the crypts, not seeing anything more recent than a decade back. "Especially when you consider the distance between inner city D.C. and out here in Nowhere Town, Maryland."

"You're trying to make sense out of a very disturbed individual's decision-making skills."

"I'd say you just described our jobs to a T." He stepped closer to Sid Waller's gaping crypt. Chunks of the cement facing were scattered around the tile flooring, but the space itself was empty.

Sixty-two-year-old Sid Waller's remains—headless as they were—had been taken away as evidence, along with the coffin.

"Our unsub had to be strong." Denae bent and peered into the space. "Pulling the coffin out couldn't have been easy."

Leo crouched beside her, staring into the crypt. "And no room in there for anything but a coffin, so they didn't get in and push it out either. I don't even know how they'd manage to get any leverage. This is so tight."

Denae stepped to the mausoleum entrance and called out to Macintosh, who was sawing at a juniper bush. "Any idea how a person would get a coffin out of a crypt if they were alone?"

The man stopped sawing and shook his head. "Haven't the foggiest. Ain't that your job to figure out? Maybe they turned into the Hulk, for all I know."

Denae turned back to the mausoleum interior. "Helpful, isn't he?"

Leo met Denae's scowl with a shrug. "There's no telling what they had for tools, I guess. They had a duffel bag, right? Maybe they used something small and mechanical to move the coffin...industrial robots? Roombas engineered for extra weight? Who the hell knows?"

"This case gets weirder and weirder." She sighed, her gaze back on Ed Macintosh, who'd returned to massacring the juniper bush.

"He seems harmless enough." Leo kept his voice low, between the two of them. "But we can't rule him out just yet. May need to bring him in for questioning...later?"

"Later." She pressed some curls back behind her ear, a motion he'd noticed she made whenever she wanted to focus. "I wouldn't say he's particularly suspect. Why report something if you did it? But most people don't seem capable of crypt robbing and head chopping. Generally speaking."

"And yet." Leo glanced back into the space of the crypt, reminding himself of the crime scene photos showing the head of bartender Jay South on Sid Waller's shrunken body. "Somebody did this."

He moved past Denae, calling it quits on the scene for the both of them.

They thanked their resident groundskeeper with a handshake. Leo handed the man a business card, requesting a call if he thought of anything else.

Macintosh returned to mishandling the shrubbery.

Heading off toward the front entrance, Leo walked close to Denae and tried to ignore the lurking sense that the gravestones were judging him as he passed.

"I looked Sid up." He walked as fast as the uneven, root-riddled ground would allow. "Apparently, the man was a convict who died in prison. I don't know if his delinquent past explains anything, but we need to check into it."

"It's possible." Denae bent to pick up a plastic bag that had blown in from nowhere and stuffed the trash into her pocket. Even in a barren cemetery, she didn't like litter. "Jay South's younger brother is in prison. Emma is on her way there right now to interview him and see if there's a connection."

"I don't know how much good an inmate who's grieving his newly dead brother can do us, but I guess it's worth a shot."

Much as anything else we've got so far anyway.

Denae grunted. "I imagine Emma'll manage to find a connection if there's one to be found."

Leo couldn't disagree with her on that point. Emma's drive and energy were freaking relentless. Not to mention exhausting.

He wrestled the wrought iron fencing open and ushered Denae through, thrilled to see the Explorer still there, waiting on their return.

Cemeteries were for dead people. He might often work for the dead, but he wasn't ready to join them.

12

Emma held Paul South's gaze as he was led into the small visitation room and seated at the table across from her. Neither of them reacted in any fashion when the guard cuffed his hands to the table and gave the usual instructions.

The rules for prisoner visits were simple. No transfer of materials or written information, no physical contact, and the first call for prisoner removal—by either party—would be heeded immediately.

With the instructions delivered, the guard stalked from the room, leaving Emma sitting across from Paul South, their first victim's younger brother and only living relative.

From beneath a ridge of buzzed blond hair, the thirty-five-year-old stared at her with more malice than Emma had seen come from anyone since the ghost of Bud Darl, a sexual predator, in Little Clementine.

Paul's sneer was impressive, even for a Metropolitan Transition Center inmate who couldn't behave—the man was nearly four years into a three-year sentence.

His eyes narrowed when she didn't speak up right away. "Out with it. What the fuck you want, Fed?"

"I'm Special Agent Emma Last. I'm here about your brother, Jay South."

"And why the fuck you think I'd talk to a Fed about him or anything else?" The man spit down at the table, but the fact he didn't spit at her directly was its own little gesture of respect. He might be a bad thief, but he wasn't stupid.

She expected a bit more of a reaction upon mentioning his brother, though. A flash of concern, maybe? Neutral-faced, she leaned forward. "You don't want us to find your brother's murderer?"

Blood drained from his face, and his tongue darted out to lick his lips. Years ago, she might have read the reaction for fear, but she wasn't a new agent any longer. This was shock. Mixed, maybe, with sudden and serious grief.

"You didn't know?" She asked just quietly enough that he'd hear her, without the guard outside being a part of the conversation.

They couldn't even tell him his brother died? He really must've made enemies of the guards around here.

One sideways jerk of the head confirmed as much. He blinked hard, and for a moment, Emma thought the man might shed a few tears. Jaw clenched, he pulled himself up straight in his chair hard enough to jingle his chains, drawing the guard's eye, and scowled anew. "How?"

Emma sighed, wishing she hadn't been the one to break the news. Shock wouldn't make this conversation any easier. "I'm sorry, Paul, I'm not at liberty to say. And I'm also sorry for the oversight. You should've been informed of Jay's death. I'd thought next of kin would've been told by now. But I'm hoping you can help me narrow down why Jay would've been a target."

Paul's eyes rolled in a fashion that might've been designed

to fight back tears or be deemed as disregard. At the same time, he didn't call for the guard to come get him, which was something.

"As his sibling, maybe you know of any bad blood Jay could've had with others. Ex-friends, business acquaintances, competitors, anyone. If you do, and you're willing to talk to me about it, you may just help us get justice for your brother."

Paul brought his eyes back to hers and leaned forward over his fisted hands. "What do you think I'd know about anything, *Agent*? I'm in fucking prison, and my brother didn't exactly come and visit me on the regular. I don't know nothin', and I couldn't help you solve shit even if I wanted to. Bastards round here didn't even tell me he was dead, and now you want my help? Man, fuck that."

Maybe Leo was right, and this was a losing endeavor, but she was already here. It couldn't hurt to press. "Well, what kind of a man was your brother?"

Paul snickered, leaning back in his chair, and spitting to the side this time. "He was an asshole. I hated the motherfucker. You want the truth? Jay probably got himself killed and deserved everything that came to him, that's what. Never knew how to make the most of what he had in that bar job, that's for sure." He raised his voice loud enough to be heard outside. "Still, would've been nice if one of these dickheads told me my own motherfucking brother was dead!"

This is getting us nowhere fast.

Paul was only getting angrier as they sat here, and more and more indignant as the shock shifted to grief and upset. Justified anger or not, she'd have to quell the emotion in the room if she hoped for any use to this visit.

"All right, Paul, well, what are you in here for? May as well talk to me while I'm here, right? Maybe we can help each other."

The man raised one ragged eyebrow at her. "Taking that direction, huh? Okay, I'll play. I'm in for grand theft, as if you didn't know." He laughed, hard and long. "I'm a thief, and I've always been a thief. Simple as that."

Emma forced a smile. "Why?"

If nothing else, maybe seeing into this man'll help me see into his brother.

"'Cause when you grow up shit-poor and you get real hungry, you get fuckin' creative about solving your problems. You pick up new skills where ya have to." He all but growled at her. "You ever gone hungry before? Ever felt your stomach start to eat itself 'cause there wasn't nothin' else for it to gnaw on?"

Emma pressed her tongue to the top of her mouth, holding in both retort and apology. There had never been a day in her life where she went hungry, or cold, or without a roof. Paul South would never understand the privilege she grew up with, or all the money in her bank account she'd inherited from her father. Her private school education was a different world from anything the man in front of her must have experienced.

Paul kept staring.

Swallowing against the guilty lump forming in her throat, she answered simply and honestly. "No, I don't know what that's like."

"Well, that's why you're on that side of the table. That's the only reason why."

"You don't think that's simplifying things a bit?" Emma sat back in her chair, crossing one leg over the other. She might've been privileged, but things weren't so black and white as Paul would have her believe. "I'd like to believe there are plenty of other reasons why I'm not in prison."

Paul rolled his eyes again, and for just a moment, Emma glimpsed a world of grief. In a moment, though, the image was gone, and the toughened convict was seated across from her once again.

"Lady, there's one thing that stands between criminals like me and upstanding individuals like you. You can see it in that fancy suit you're wearing, if you want to. It's money. If you started over as a piss-poor baby in a trailer, you'd understand fast. People on my side of the bars get it. Some people aren't born with a chance in hell. They're just born into it."

"And what about your brother?" Emma pointed out. "He wasn't behind bars, and he must've come from the same beginnings as you, right?"

Paul gave a crooked grin, eyes going soft in a way that made him look ten years older than he was. "Well, yeah, but use your head. Why do you think that is, huh? Two kids from the same dirt-poor patch of concrete end up in two separate spots. Somebody in the family had to sacrifice in order for that to happen. Fat load of good it did me. Or him, apparently."

The words came like a punch in the gut. Paul had found a way to help his brother, at his own expense, and ended up in prison. Whether he hated Jay or not. And now his brother was dead and gone anyway.

At a rare loss for words, Emma could only watch as Paul yelled for a guard and proclaimed that he was done with the visit.

He blustered at the guard as he left the room, spitting at the man's boots and making a show of threatening legal action over not being told about his brother. Though everyone knew there'd be no such lawsuit. Paul was a nobody locked into a hole.

Maybe his brother hadn't been much better off.

Sitting for another moment, Emma rose only when a second guard showed up to escort her back outside. Unease had settled in her gut. She couldn't help being acutely aware of the soft rub of her silk blouse within her warm coat. Her slacks didn't rustle like cheap fabric would, and her boots had soft soles that kept her feet mostly happy even after a long day. Paul was right that she'd never known poverty. She'd never done without when it came to material things at all.

The prison was chilly and dark, but walking back out into the sunshine somehow didn't help.

A hollow, rotten feeling ran through her blood. Guilt.

For the first time, she was glad Jacinda had headed back to the office. Emma hated that her supervisor didn't feel all that well—hopefully her stomach had settled by now—but Paul South had put her off her game.

Her own privilege loomed over her, and Emma didn't care to have company while she pushed past the sensation.

At her back, the penitentiary cast long shadows, somehow seeming related to the inner-city graveyard she'd visited earlier.

Both locations were hard, forgotten places housing hard, forgotten souls…

13

Mia blinked, focusing against the glare of her computer screen. The video footage of the parking lot of the convenience store closest to Angel Willows Cemetery was dim. She watched as a child, about five years old, climbed sleepily back into his parents' minivan. They belted him in then climbed into the front. This family was the first traffic for half an hour.

She sighed, turning to Vance. "Are we done here?"

"Yeah. We're not getting anywhere, and we're already out of the window when our unsub would've stopped at this rest stop. You want coffee?"

"At six in the evening, are you kidding?" She laughed and shook out her short hair, trying to shake herself awake. "Not unless Jacinda wants us to pull an all-nighter for some reason."

Vance stood, stretching in a way that only reminded her how lean and well-built he was. Then walked away, tossing her a wink over his shoulder.

That stretch was intentional, damn him!

Mia held in a giggle and shut down her laptop. The act of

closing the lid reminded her how futile the last few hours' work had proved to be—combing through CCTV footage from a Maryland rest stop and coming up with nothing.

A soft ding indicated the elevator had arrived, and Mia looked up. Emma exited, stepping into the narrow foyer that divided the bullpen from the elevator and stairwell access. She smiled as she spotted Mia. "Any luck?"

Mia grimaced. "CCTV didn't come through with anything. Only some fairly boring numbers." She lifted her notepad. "For example, on the night Jay South's head was placed on Sid Waller's body, *thirty-seven* vehicles headed north on that highway. *Eleven* of them after dark. *Three* of them after midnight and technically on the thirtieth of January rather than the twenty-ninth."

Emma laughed at her emphasis on the numbers. "That's precise."

"Exactly." Mia stretched in her chair, dropping the notebook back on her desk. "Even the few visible faces belonged to families with small children. Not even remotely worth wasting our time on."

"Damn." Emma muttered to herself, leaning against the desk. "So I guess a license plate is too much to hope for?"

Mia shot her a reproachful glance, telling Emma she should know better with a single look. "Better believe it. No license plates or anything else that could help. Just blurry vehicles and their approximate colors."

Vance stepped out of the break room just as Jacinda exited her office and headed toward the conference room. "Come one, come all, folks. Time for a breakdown."

Emma took a chair near one end of the table. She slid her laptop in front of her and peered at her screen with a frown.

Mia dropped into the seat next to Emma, and the smile she received in return eased her nerves just a little. Emma had been acting so oddly that morning, but she seemed to be on a more even keel since getting back from the prison.

More reserved than usual, perhaps…but Mia would take that any day over the unpredictable, erratic behavior from the morning.

"Emma, can you put the security footage up on the projector?" Jacinda grabbed the seat at the front of the table and pulled her chair to the side just a bit so they could all face the screen she'd pulled down.

Leo dimmed the light.

The SSA still wasn't feeling well. Mia almost never saw Jacinda sit down.

"What you're all seeing is the footage Detective Danielson sent over from Van Der Beek Cemetery."

Emma hit play, and the screen showed scratchy footage of a masked individual pushing through the gates. She narrated what they were witnessing. "They entered at roughly two in the morning and left at closer to three thirty." Slowing the tape, Emma zoomed in on the figure and replayed the entrance.

Mia squinted, focusing on Emma's laptop rather than the enlarged screen at the front of the room. "Wait…go back. I saw something."

Emma rewound, and Mia rushed to hit the pause button when the screen showed their unsub halfway through the gate, their duffel pressed slightly against the metal fencing.

At the front of the room, Mia pointed to a round bulge in the bag. On the big screen it looked like the duffel bag had bulged out a bit on one side, making it look uneven. "You all see this? Are you thinking what I'm thinking?"

Jacinda let out a breath. "I think so. Good catch, Agent Logan."

Denae leaned forward, stretching across the table, trying

to get closer to the big screen. "Catch the rest of us up, Mia. What are you seeing?"

Mia went to the big screen and pointed to the round shape visible against the bag's fabric. "Round, as much space as this takes up? What do you want to bet this was Terry Derby's head?"

Leo tapped a pen on the table, and Mia resisted the urge to put her hand over his. The thudding was irritating. "And Marcus Peabody's head when they left. We find that bag, we can probably find some DNA to tie the killer to the bodies."

Peering back at the image, Mia focused on the shape and tried to internalize the image. Black duffels were common, but if she spotted someone connected to their victims carrying one, she didn't want to miss it.

Emma set the video to play again. "Figure appears slight enough that we could be looking for a woman or a very small man."

"As long as they're fit and strong." Mia leaned forward, watching the way the person moved as Emma played and replayed the recording. "Does that fit any…well, no, do we have any suspects?"

She'd spoken to the table at large, but her colleagues remained focused on the screen for another moment before anyone commented.

And when the recap came, it didn't offer much, let alone a suspect.

Aside from the strand of hair found near Peabody's crypt, and the security footage they'd just viewed, nothing significant had come of the day's investigation. Even if their suspect was a woman, as the surveillance suggested, they couldn't say for sure there wasn't a partner, or partners, involved.

Leo closed the cover of his iPad with a sigh as Emma shut down the footage. "We don't have much. I did finally make headway on Terry Derby's phone records. They should be getting sent over by tomorrow morning, and maybe that'll crack the case wide open so—"

"Or," Vance flipped on the lights, "just tell us he was interacting with a party who was using a burner phone. If they've got a brain, that is."

Jacinda strung fingers through her hair, her eyes on the blank projector screen. "Everyone, go home and get some rest. Make sure to jot down any more theories or ideas that come to you tonight. We'll meet at eight sharp, and I'll dole out assignments."

For a moment, Mia thought to follow Emma as her friend hightailed it out of the conference room, Jacinda near on her heels. She held off, though, and waited for Vance to finish a quiet conversation with Leo instead.

Truthfully, she had no desire to repeat her conversation with Emma from that morning or have more cause to dwell on her brother.

For just a moment, Ned's smiling face eclipsed everything else in the room. The same expression as when they'd passed their driver's license exams, graduated high school, then college…and enjoyed so many of each other's birthday celebrations. That was how she wanted to remember him.

Not the way he'd looked after his accident, when she'd had to identify his body.

A shiver ran through her, shoving her out of the memory and back into real life. She couldn't let Ned's death keep derailing her like this, in odd moments, just because his name came up in conversation.

No, she didn't want to think about Ned right now. Since there was nothing she could do about the situation, it was better to focus on what was in front of her. She hoped to completely escape thoughts of her dead brother…at least for the night.

Better to just wait and try to lure Vance out for a nice meal, taking them both away from the case and the stress of the job.

Ned would want her to be happy, right? Not dwelling on him. Just happy.

And she was capable of that. She had to be.

14

Snuggling beneath a blanket on her couch, Emma could almost forget about the headless bodies and bodiless heads making up her current case.

Almost.

Lemon-ginger tea, lovely as it was, only went so far.

Her phone jolted her from the couch before she remembered someone other than work could be calling. Sure enough, Jacinda's icon was not the one showing on her smartphone.

Instead, the contact information for the Yoga Map greeted her, and the owner's handsome smiling face flashed immediately to mind. Oren Werling.

Couldn't hurt to talk to a normal person, Emma girl. At least for a little while.

She muted the television and brought the phone to her ear. "Hello?"

"Emma, I'm so glad you picked up. It's Oren Werling, from the Yoga Map. How are you?"

His lilting voice fluttered something in her belly. "I'm

fine…kinda wondering if you're a stalker, though. Little late for business hours?"

He laughed. "I didn't mark you for an early-to-bed type. And it's not nine yet. Besides, I didn't force you to put your number on the registration card at the studio, did I?"

Meeting questions with questions. He's either trying to be mysterious…or he likes me.

That flutter got faster as she considered those blue eyes that watched her—in a good way—when she made her laughable attempts at yoga poses.

She glanced at the clock. Eight fifty. Definitely past business hours. "So is this an important yoga-related call, then? Considering the time? A yoga-mergency?"

Hearing the joke out loud made Emma cringe into her couch.

Please laugh, please laugh.

When he did, the lightness of the sound loosened something in her. Muscles relaxed. Every instinct insisted she lean back and just enjoy the moment. Like the moments when she heard a favorite song and forgot about her job and the evil that people were capable of.

She did want to see more of this man, and not just in the studio.

"Yes and no, we'll say? I admit, I usually wait a bit longer to check in with someone who came for one class…but I was thinking about you today. Figured if I waited for you to come to another yoga session, I might never get to ask you out at all. Or lose my nerve."

The breath caught in Emma's chest. She'd been flirting, yeah…but she hadn't expected him to ask her out. Not really. A handsome, charming business owner who'd met her once? Not to mention she'd been attracted to him from the start too.

"Emma? Are you there?"

"I...yeah. Sorry." She blinked back to the moment and sat a little straighter. "You just caught me off guard."

"In a good way, I hope? So...what's the outlook for a first date in a spiffy federal agent's schedule?"

"Wow...uh...well..." She stopped, her voice lost again, for the second time in a day. Did she really want to start a relationship with someone new? Even a serious flirtation? Right now? *But you like him, Emma girl, even if you've only met him once.* "Honestly, Oren, my schedule's packed as hell...but I would love to. It's just a question of timing."

"I'll take that as a positive?" The lilt in his voice was teasing, not put off as she feared...and it cemented her interest. If he could give her space, another box checked in his favor. "How about you give me a call when you get a breather from work? I'll text you my personal number."

"I'd like that."

"And, hey there, don't forget...yoga offers more than a few benefits when it comes to dealing with a stressful career. The studio is here when you're ready to come back and get a class in, date notwithstanding."

Emma's phone pinged, signaling his personal number had just come through. "I've got your number, promise. And... hey, thanks for calling."

"Thank you for picking up. Good night."

"Good night." Emma ended the call and stared at her phone for a few seconds. *Talk about unexpected.*

Over the weekend, Keaton had asked if anyone new had caught her eye lately. She'd hesitated, but Oren had definitely come to mind.

Maybe this was a sign.

A very different kind of sign from those offered by inhabitants of the Other.

At the thought of signs, and ghosts, Emma glanced around her apartment, but the space was blissfully clear. Her one regular visitor would likely be back in the morning, like clockwork, but the second part of her day had been clearer of ghosts than she'd expected after the whirlwind beginning.

Or maybe you're just getting better at tuning them out?

That was a definite possibility.

But one ghost stuck out to her from that day.

Pushing Oren's call from her mind, Emma thought back to the young ghost in the fancy dress she'd seen at the Van Der Beek Cemetery. She sipped at the remains of her lukewarm tea, considering. There'd been a lot of law enforcement around…could the girl have appeared for a reason, but been scared off early?

"Maybe she does have something to say. Something that matters."

Emma's muttering in the silence of her apartment decided the matter. If she was going to talk to herself, and potentially summon ghosts, she ought to try to communicate with a spirit that could make a difference.

Not bothering to put on anything more formal than the sweatpants and long-sleeved t-shirt she already wore, Emma pulled on her coat and headed out the door. Not for the first time, she patted herself on the back for never breaking down and moving out to the suburbs. Van Der Beek Cemetery was no more than fifteen minutes away.

Amazing how close the worst side of town always seems to be in a city. Not a bad thing tonight anyway.

By the time she'd parked and locked her Prius, Emma's better senses had chimed in. A nighttime trip to inner-city D.C. was one more sign she'd lost her mind. But it was too late to change her plans. Not without feeling like a fool to herself.

Her flashlight beam flickered along the graves as she walked the cemetery's pathways. Step-by-step she avoided mud puddles and broken pavers between headstones.

Feeling like an idiot, she kept her voice low and called for the ghost. "Little girl? Are you here? Was there something you wanted to tell me?"

This was ridiculous. She sounded like a crazy cat lady calling for her kitties.

Ghosts talk to me when they want, on their dime. I can't summon them.

This was a useless plan, if it could even be called a plan, but she was already there. Another few minutes couldn't hurt anything but her pride.

"Little girl! Can you hear me? We saw each other earlier—"

A blast of icy air hit Emma.

The girl in the blue Easter dress, complete with a hole in her chest, appeared directly in Emma's path, just a few feet away. Emma yelped and fell backward, landing on her ass in the cold grass. The white gaze of the child ghost didn't react to Emma's embarrassment.

"Shit. Sorry. I mean, crap. Didn't mean to curse."

Shit, why are you apologizing to a ghost? She's older than you at this point. Get it together.

Even as her heart kept trying to beat out of her chest, Emma scrambled to her feet, picking up her flashlight from where it'd fallen in the muck. Brushing mud from her coat and sweatpants, she grimaced at the sensation of the soil on her hands. Her palm burned where she'd scraped against a cement paver. So much for grace under fire.

But the girl was here now, and Emma would make the most of it.

The girl's blue dress was dressier than Emma had realized, trimmed with fancy white lace and fluffed into an A-line that would have done any bridesmaid proud. Emma inched forward, coming to within arm's reach of the child and working up a smile. "I like your dress."

The ghost's head cocked sideways, as if calling her on the small talk.

Touché.

"Okay...so the thing is...I'm just a friend. My name's Emma, and I'm trying to catch someone who did something very bad. I'm hoping you can help me?"

The girl remained frozen for so long that Emma nearly jumped when the child finally lifted one delicate hand to point to her own chest. Directly at the hole a large-caliber shotgun had blasted into her at some distant point in the past.

Emma swallowed, nodding. Violence didn't normally bother her, even this close, but it was different to see such a gruesome injury on a person who was also moving around. And Emma had hoped that the girl hadn't been aware of her own terrible wound. She guessed souls couldn't live in bliss while carrying around the gore every day in the Other, though.

"That's right. Like that. Maybe you saw something last night in the cemetery that seemed...wrong?"

The girl licked her lips, shifting on her feet. Her white eyes couldn't focus anywhere, but the pinched appearance of her cheeks suggested they would've been avoiding Emma's eyes either way. Emma had almost given up on the ghost speaking by the time her lips opened, voice wavering as she spoke.

"The lady wasn't bad." The girl dug one saddle shoe into the mud, twisting the toe nervously. "Trying to save. He wanted the lady to leave with him, too, but her ears don't hear."

Was it too much to ask for the girl to name the *she* and the *he* here? Emma was just about to ask, when the girl stiffened, her head turning so fast that her brown hair swung out with the wind.

"What's wr—"

"They're here!" She began backing away from Emma, fast. "Run!"

Too stunned to move for a full second, Emma couldn't bring herself to speak until the girl had disappeared.

And then the nebulous "they" registered like a strobe light in her brain.

Without bothering to turn and try to see what the girl had seen, Emma darted across the grass and swerved toward the entrance. She ran at a full sprint, willing her steps to remain sure. Her heart pounded, but she didn't allow herself to slow down, even as she fished her car keys from her coat pocket and swung out of the cemetery's entrance.

The key fob beeped, opening the lock, just as Emma yanked on the car handle and dove inside, slamming the door. She jammed the push start, wanting to get the hell out of this place.

Damn the Other and damn her own hide for being so scared.

But, seriously, the time to face down her fears wasn't after dark in a cemetery in the middle of inner-city D.C.

Not by the longest of shots.

Giving her car more gas, she slammed her hand against the steering wheel and worked to slow her racing heartbeat. The girl had spoken to her, at least. She had to focus on that bit of good news.

Even if the Other chased her down and treated her like prey, Emma would be damned if she'd drop down in a grave and cooperate in the effort. *Screw that.* Whatever was coming, she'd face up to it soon.

But on her terms.

15

Rick Royer shook his leg, sending a moth flying off his jeans. It fluttered away into the cold night sky. Even the unseasonal little pest couldn't ruin Rick's good mood. In fact, he could play the unknowing chauffeur to another dozen moths—which he might have to, this far out into rural Maryland—and still be grinning.

Holly, the prettiest woman he'd met in ages, was waiting inside this house. She made most of his other affairs look like warmed-over crap on a shoe, and she'd promised a homemade dinner by candlelight.

Granted, she might not have agreed to the night's meeting if she'd known he was married, but she hadn't figured that out. At least, not yet.

He gave the land a once-over. There was money behind this house. Beyond the home, a well-kept greenhouse, the romantic location for this evening's dinner, stood bright and shiny. Glass panes glowed with artificial light.

The whole scene was idyllic, much better than the seedy motels he normally frequented.

His wife expected motel receipts as part of his business

expenses, but no way would he let some insect-infested rathole get in the way of giving Holly a few good rides on his pogo stick.

Married! Crap.

He'd nearly forgotten to take off his friggin' ring.

He pulled the jewelry from his finger, walked back to his car, and tucked it into the glove box. A small bottle of aftershave sat at the bottom of the compartment.

"May as well." With a spray against his neck and armpits, he figured he was about ready. He slammed the car door and stretched, trying to get the nervous jitters out.

Relax. Holly's interested in you, not the thread count of your sheets. Women don't make dinner for men they're not interested in.

"Beautiful, and sweet as pie too," he muttered to himself. Speaking of pie, he hoped she'd made dessert, as well. Would be a nice post-sex treat.

He wandered down the lawn toward the greenhouse. Candles flickered alongside the artificial lights. Tall flowers made it hard for him to see the interior. The door to the greenhouse was open, and he felt the warm, moist air trickling out, carrying the scent of garlic and tomatoes.

Precisely at nine, he stood at the greenhouse entrance and called her name. "Holly?"

A woman with gorgeous dark hair flowing over her shoulders stood in the doorway. Bright red lips smiled at him. "Hi."

He grinned wide. "Hi yourself."

Just as pretty as advertised in her profile, she had long gams, clad in curve-hugging leggings, and a short skirt that showed them off along with a loose blouse that itself would have made him salivate, even without the smell of lasagna following her outside. Her shining blue eyes just about melted him when she offered a cheeky smile.

"Rick, it's so good to meet you." She stepped forward and

looped both her arms around his neck, bumping her nose against his before pulling back and taking his hand. "Welcome. Come on in."

She led him into the greenhouse. Her grasp was firm, but her hands were soft. He could imagine what those hands could do…

A small table was set up in the rear corner. Bright purple flowers dominated a whole corner of the space. "Pretty."

"Thank you."

"I meant the flowers, but, yes, you too."

Holly laughed. She bent over the casserole dish at the center of the table, lifting the corners of the cover.

"Oh, let me handle it. You've already slaved over a hot stove."

Acting the knight, Rick opened the casserole dish and took up the serving spoon. He gallantly filled their plates. He should have brought some wine, though. The sauce smelled delicious, and a nice red would've rounded that out.

Maybe next time.

He took a whiff of her hair as he set her food in front of her.

"Is that lavender perfume I smell on top of lasagna?"

"You've got a good nose." She blushed, licking her upper lip.

Holy heaven.

Rick's stomach growled as he filled his own plate. He wasn't sure if it was hunger or desire. "You've outdone yourself. I'm so glad you agreed to meet in person. What a beautiful idea."

"I feel the same." Holly leaned forward, offering him a pointed glimpse of her best assets, and his throat dried. This woman put his other affairs to shame. "Shall we eat, and… well…" she stammered, laughing, then peered up at him with a red-lipped smile that just about did him in, "see where the night leads us?"

Rick swallowed, barely finding his voice. "Please." The plea was for more than dinner. At the moment, his mind spun, and he couldn't think of any combo better than a belly full of pasta followed by a hot younger woman on his dick.

He almost startled when another moth made an appearance on his shirtsleeve. He extended his arm to the side and gave it a shake, sending the moth flapping off just like the first one. The creepy creature must've been confused by the greenhouse heat. It would probably find its way back later on, but that would be okay. He'd just escort it off his person, so he could concentrate on getting closer to Holly's person.

Her fingers touched his arm, and he turned to see her looking at him with wide eyes and the brightest smile he'd ever seen.

"You're really a good man, Rick, aren't you? So caring, even for the smallest living things."

"I guess. Moths, bugs, even spiders…they all want to live, just like the rest of us. Sometimes they get in the wrong place, is all."

She began cutting her food into bite-size pieces. He wondered out loud if maybe they ought to relax and get comfortable first? She shook her head and emitted a little *tsk* that reminded him of a sexy librarian he'd seen in a porn flick a few nights back.

"I want you to enjoy the lasagna while it's hot. Trust me, you'll think it's to die for, and after that, we'll have the rest of the night together. Just us."

He focused on her lips and delicate hands, barely listening to her yammer on about her day. "Whatever you say."

He took a bite and adjusted himself, trying to pretend he wasn't hard.

If she noticed, she didn't say anything, only smiling and showing off her dimples.

Twisting open a water bottle for herself, she watched as he made a show of loading up his fork and enjoying a big, cheesy bite. She wanted to watch him eat, that was fine by him…maybe she didn't want to fill herself up before the action. Women had a thing about that.

The lasagna was different from his wife's, but not bad. Little bit of a nutty aftertaste, but he swept up some sauce and took a quick, second, third, then fourth ginormous bite, ready for the meal after the meal.

"How's it taste?"

Before he could breathe out a response, his heart went haywire.

Pounding and erratic, the damn organ just about blurred the world in front of his eyes. His mouth gaped, searching for the air to tell his date what was happening. As if from a distance, he watched his hand fumble for purchase on the table, numb and useless.

Choking, he fell sideways onto the brick path.

Another moth swam through the air in front of his face, making its awkward path up and up, away from him and toward the lights above.

Oh, god. I'm having a heart attack.

Chest tight and burning, he rolled onto his back, barely aware of his head scraping the pavers or his knee knocking aside the chair. His lips stretched, aching for breath.

Holly was above him…standing and looking down on him. Watching. And…smiling.

"Don't worry." She crouched, and if not for the leggings, he could have seen up her skirt, but for the first time in his life, he didn't care. He couldn't breathe. "It'll all be over soon, and I've got the perfect place for you to rest."

He flopped a hand up and against his chest, unable to feel

his limbs. What was this woman talking about? What was going on?

What did this crazy bitch just feed me? What did I eat? We didn't even get to screw!

She grinned wider, as if reading the question in his mind.

Broken breaths seized his throat. He gaped, a blinding pain gripping him and arching his body against the floor, stabbing at every inch of him as his heart pounded.

The pressure in his chest increased, and he realized he would never get this force, this monstrous weight, off him.

His wife's face flashed before his eyes. Barb was an ER nurse. He'd once watched her save a man from choking in a restaurant. While the rest of the diners panicked, she'd calmly walked over, wrapped her sturdy arms around the choking man, and squeezed until the olive pit flew out of his throat.

Barb hadn't broken a sweat. Her fine features remained steady. That was the face he saw now, as if she were telling him to calm down.

But the pressure built.

He couldn't catch his breath.

Barb leaned over him, and she wasn't calm and steady now. No, there was something *greedy* as she bent near his face. He could feel her breath on his cheek.

In horror, he watched as his wife's dark skin paled and paled, fading to a ghastly white except for those scarlet lips.

Barb had never been here.

The last thing he heard was the words from those bloodred lips. "Thank you."

16

Newly dressed in jeans and one of Michael's old sweatshirts, I drove Ricky's car down to the lakeside, right where I'd disposed of Terry Derby's used body. The drop-off here was deep enough for four cars stacked vertically, at least. And I couldn't have anyone find Rick's ride.

I was going on forty-two hours of no sleep, and the manic excitement I'd felt earlier was fast fading into muscle fatigue. If only Michael could help me...

But I promised I'd be with him, awake, through this whole rejuvenation, and I meant it. I can do this. Three days without sleep is nothing compared to an eternity with my soulmate.

My breath burned with the acrid odor of coffee, and I could feel it churning in my stomach. It was only the second day of our ritual, and I had downed so many mugs of the bitter brew. I wanted to throw up after drinking the last cup this afternoon. But I knew it would sustain me through the trials ahead.

Giving Michael a fast smile, I released the parking brake and stepped behind the car. There was a slight incline into the lake, so the car rolled obediently down, splashing into the black water. I'd rolled all the windows down. The sinking process didn't take long. A heavy, satisfying squelching sound signaled the vehicle had fully disappeared beneath the surface.

"Coming to get you, Ricky."

He still lay on the ground by the table, red sauce dribbled down his chin and his chest as if he were a toddler.

A shame to see him like this. He'd seemed nice…if a little too eager. That worked in my favor tonight, though. His horniness meant he was blind to dangers.

I moved my wheelbarrow right up beside him and got my hands under his armpits, ready to heft his limp form. I paused when I spotted a lighter band of skin around the third finger on his left hand.

He was married. Or he had been until very recently.

Did I choose wrong? No, no, no, it can't be wrong. It can't be. He has to be right. He has to be a good man. Like Michael.

I thought back to what I'd learned about Ricky when we chatted online. He traveled for work a lot. He sold office supplies for a distributor that shipped nationwide.

"You never mentioned being married, Ricky. You never told me you had a wife."

Maybe he didn't. Maybe that was why he'd been so eager and so horny. He must've been married at one time, and his career kept him away from home so much that his wife asked for a divorce.

That had to be it. He was lonely and a little desperate. But even good men could get lonely.

My fatigue wore on me, and I fought the urge to sit down instead of getting on with the work. Time was not on my side, and I still had the onerous task of placing Ricky's head where it belonged.

Gripping him under his arms, I hauled him up to an

awkward sitting position. Luckily, rigor mortis took a while to set in. I had time.

Still, he was heavy. I stretched my back, got my legs under me, and rose, bringing Ricky with me so that he stood like a scarecrow leaning against me. With two careful steps, I rotated him to face me and walked us over, so we stood between the wheelbarrow's handles. Now he'd fall into it on his backside instead of smashing his face. I gave myself a second once he was situated, before letting him slump into the wheelbarrow.

It trembled under him, and I had to grab the handles to prevent it from toppling to one side and spilling him onto the floor again.

"Talk about dead weight. And you didn't need that pasta dinner, buddy."

Michael gave me a thumbs-up of approval. I blew him a kiss and started wheeling Rick outside, where the bloody part of the evening's festivities could begin.

"Now for the hard part." I glanced up at Michael, who leaned on the greenhouse doorjamb. *Bless him.* "Wanna help?"

He frowned. "I'm sorry, love. I wish I could. Just think of what's coming to us."

I took strength from the fact that he was more willing to speak to me. That had to mean I was right about Ricky. He hadn't been married. He'd been a good man after all, and so caring for that harmless and helpless moth too. I just knew he was perfect for this part of our ritual.

Ricky was about my height, but pudgier instead of lean and muscular. His online pictures had not been recent, as I'd also tried to choose men that I knew I could manage physically. My arms ached as I struggled to control the wheelbarrow down the hill.

The sight was obscene, with his head, arms, and lower legs still bouncing outside the wheelbarrow's confines.

Once I'd gotten him to the grassy spot where I'd laid my tools, including a hurricane lantern that cast the whole scene in flickering orange light—almost romantic—I'd be fine.

Time to take him out. I stretched my sore arms, but nothing seemed to relieve the ache.

I took aim at his shoulders first, and on the count of three, lifted with every bit of push-up strength I'd gained over the last three years of preparing for just this sort of moment.

When I had him halfway up, the wheelbarrow overcorrected, and I lost my grip. Ricky flopped out as it hit the grass. He landed in a clumsy tangle of limp arms and legs.

I grabbed under his armpits again—man, did this guy stink of cologne!—wrapped my arms around his chest, and tugged him clear of the wheelbarrow.

Every one of my muscles complained, but I almost felt a little buzzed from the effort. High on life, as my mom would have said, and as Michael had so often echoed.

"Look, Michael, we did it!"

Michael waved at me from the cliff, checking that the car had fully disappeared. "Don't forget to clean up, love."

Right, right, right.

Gloves on. These were thick leather, which meant I'd have more protection from the teeth of the saw.

But I'd discovered it was a bit easier to start with the hatchet.

The saw, the hatchet, and a hammer and chisel glinted in the lantern light.

With Terry Derby, I'd removed his head in the bathtub in the house, thinking it was easier to clean. However, bleaching and cleaning took *forever*. And carrying his dead weight all the way out to the greenhouse...that was not a task I wanted to repeat. So with Ricky, I planned to remove his head next to the lake, dump him immediately, then use the garden hose to rinse off any excess…*liquids*.

Swallowing hard, I rolled him onto his stomach, then picked up the hatchet. Two or three good whacks to the back of the neck would break through the spine.

I lifted the tool and brought it down as hard as I could.

Almost home free now.

Next came the saw. I made sure Ricky's face remained turned toward the ground. I didn't want to see his eyes staring up at me.

The night's work was hard, but I pressed through. Michael whispered encouragement when the going got really tough. But eventually, Ricky's head became fully severed from his body, and I immediately wrapped it and set it in my duffel bag. Because he was thoroughly dead, his blood didn't spray out nearly as much as if his heart were still beating. Still, I had plenty of leakage to clean up. I'd need to spray down the area with the garden hose, like I'd thought.

First, though, I wrapped and weighted Ricky's body the same as I'd done with Terry—which meant my shoulders cramped and sweat poured into my eyes by the time I was finished with that chore. Because it hurt to move, I remained on my knees and rolled the body along to the drop-off, letting gravity and momentum take him to the water.

This splash was different than with the car. A loud smack, like a belly flop, was followed by gurgling noises.

Watching the water go still, it occurred to me I could have saved so much ache and effort by simply putting Ricky in his car after removing his head.

Maybe next time.

17

Leo was ten minutes away from the VCU offices when his phone buzzed, his brother's name popping up on the Bluetooth alert of his dashboard. Speak of the devil…he'd meant to call Aleksy yesterday after talking with Denae. Then the new case had blown the thought right out of his mind.

"Aleksy! You caught me just before work." Leo slowed the truck a touch, knowing he was prone to hit the gas without thinking when distracted on the phone. "How's it going?"

"Uh, fine. But, hey, you need to know, Yaya had a fall. She's okay, but you should call her."

Dammit. "She break anything?"

"No. Maybe her pride. Mostly, she's just bruised and cranky with a sore knee. Happened last week, but I just found out she hadn't told you."

Leo unclenched his hands from the wheel, trying not to think about how old his grandmother was. She shouldn't be living alone. "Well, I'm gladder than ever that we've got a doctor in the family."

"Ha. Barely."

Barely was right. Aleksy's shift from residency to fellowship had happened only months ago. Regardless of that fact, though, he knew what he was doing, and Leo trusted his brother to tell him the lay of the land when it came to Yaya.

"And you're doing okay?" Leo made a turn a bit too fast, distracted by the silence on the line. He shouldn't be driving and talking. It wasn't safe. "All's good?"

"Just…this kind of thing, you should know. I don't think you're gonna hear about it unless I tell you. And I'll try… obviously, that's why I'm calling. You know I'm not gonna leave you out, but life gets busy here too. You should try to make a trip home once in a while."

Leo nodded even though his brother couldn't see him. "I'm gonna try—"

"You said that before you transferred. Remember?"

Yeah, he did. And he'd thought he'd have time between leaving Miami and getting settled in D.C. too. Things just hadn't quite worked out that way.

"Tell Yaya I'll call her. Would you?"

"Yeah. I will. Just remember, she's not gonna live forever, all right? You do that for me?"

Leo assured his brother he would and hurried off the line before guilt choked him up.

He hadn't asked Aleksy how long Yaya had waited for help after she'd fallen, or if she'd been alone. She had one of those emergency necklaces and could call emergency services easily.

Honestly, he didn't want to know the answers to those questions.

Yaya didn't tell him everything. He knew it, and Aleksy knew it too. Their grandmother thought they both had jobs and lives that were too stressful, with Leo's being dangerous to boot.

When she could hide her own struggles and headaches from her boys, she did.

Guilt ate at Leo's guts as he pulled into the Bureau's drive, parked, and headed up to the bullpen to the case that awaited him. As soon as this case was wrapped up, he'd start making plans for a trip home. Yaya deserved that much from him. And he'd call her sooner than that too.

Stepping out of the elevator, Leo heard Jacinda calling everyone into the conference room. He wasn't late, but in her book, on time was closer to late than not.

Last into the room after dropping his gear at his desk, Leo closed the door behind him and leaned against the wall. Jacinda seemed pale, still off her game in the sense that she appeared a little ragged and imperfect, but she stood with her usual confidence at the whiteboard, which was a step in the right direction.

"We've got another crime scene, a newly disturbed crypt." Jacinda paused, waiting to let the information sink in. "The crypt's in a different inner-city graveyard, over at Felicity Tree Cemetery. It was a companion crypt for a husband and wife."

"Jesus," Leo muttered.

Jacinda nodded. "The husband, a man named William Rigert, was the only occupant. His wife, Jessa, will need to be interviewed. Just like before, the head of another man had been placed on Rigert's body, and the recently dead victim is one Rick Royer, fifty-five years old, white male. Our unsub's third victim, from the looks of things."

Mia scribbled down details on a notepad as fast as Jacinda talked. "Fast ID."

Jacinda sighed. "We got lucky where he didn't. His wife, Barb Royer, came to the police station early this morning when her husband didn't come home last night. She thought he might've stayed at his office because of some inventory headaches. He'll occasionally sleep on a couch, but that wasn't the case."

"Mistress," Emma murmured. "I'd put money on it."

Leo wouldn't bet against her.

Jacinda ignored the comment and continued the brief. "According to her, he wasn't answering his phone. She said he always answers his phone, no matter where he is. When she called a third time and he didn't answer, she was sure something awful happened. Checked with his boss in the middle of the night, confirmed he wasn't in the office, then immediately reported it."

"Well, she was right something bad happened," Leo allowed, "but that's awfully fast…fast enough that I'd say she's now a person of interest."

Jacinda finished writing the new names up on the board and turned back to face the team. "We did get forensic results back on the strand of hair found at the previous scene, but they only confirm the hair came from a Caucasian person. Nothing more specific. Judging from the length of the hair and the size of the person we caught on video, though, if it does belong to the unsub…then, I'd say we're most likely searching for a female with long brown hair."

Emma jumped in. "Does our newly grieving widow have long brown hair?"

"She does not. Barb Royer is Black with curly hair." Jacinda sat down, her energy seeming to wane. "Meanwhile, Terry Derby's phone records have confirmed he placed several calls to a burner phone over the last two weeks."

"And his kids said they thought he was going on a date." Emma tapped her pen on the table, eyes roving over the details on the whiteboard. "If our possible unsub profile points to a brunette female, that would fit. Terry was a straight male headed out to see a woman for dinner."

The details on the board confirmed the three victims

seemed to have nothing in common aside from being heterosexual, white males who were roughly the same age. The disturbed crypts also had nothing in common.

Leo spoke up before Jacinda could dismiss everyone. "Still...the victims had to have been chosen for a reason, right? We're not just accepting that everyone on the victim list is random already?"

Jacinda pulled her red hair up into a messy bun, signaling it was time to get to business. "Absolutely not. We look for a pattern until one's ruled out. That's why I want us interviewing who we can. Sid Waller has no known relatives in the area and has been dead for fifty-some years. But the families of the other desecrated burials need to be interviewed ASAP. Also, Barb Royer provided officers with a list of women she knows her husband had affairs with—"

Vance choked on his coffee. "She had their names?"

A small smirk tilted Jacinda's lips. "Apparently. And while one of the women on the list is also deceased, two are alive and well. I want those living mistresses interviewed along with Barb Royer."

Jacinda turned back to the board, posting printed grainy pictures of the women from Rick's affairs. Both photos looked like social media profile pictures.

Emma stood almost immediately, stalking up to the board and pointing at the women one by one. "Look at this. All of them are long-haired brunettes, matching our profile. We could have our killer on this board already."

Leo leaned over the table. "Wouldn't be the first time a love story went horribly wrong—"

Lurching up from his chair, Vance sideswiped Leo's chair, cutting Leo off and turning him half around. Vance stumbled from the conference room, the door swinging wildly behind him.

Leo craned his neck sideways to glimpse the man sprinting into the men's restroom at the side of the bullpen.

Mia charged after him.

"What the hell?" Emma met Leo's eyes before turning to their SSA, but Jacinda Hollingsworth had gone white—well, whiter. She clutched her stomach, her cheeks tightening, and after another second, she threw a hand over her mouth and hightailed it from the room too.

Leo and the remaining team members hurried after their colleagues.

Denae followed Jacinda into the women's room. "Jacinda? You okay?" The door swung closed behind her.

Mia poked her head from the men's room as they approached.

"Vance is really sick, you guys. I've got quarters in my bag if someone can grab him some ginger ale from the vending machine?"

Emma hustled over to the bullpen and Mia's bag.

"Get one for Jacinda too." Leo called after her.

Seconds later, Denae stepped out of the women's room, a little green.

Leo raised one eyebrow.

She shook her head. "I'm fine...just not good at seeing others get sick. Sympathetic gag reflex and all that." She turned toward the men's room as a loud retching sound made its way past the doorway. The groan that followed couldn't be ignored.

Denae leaned back on the doorframe of the women's room. The concern was clear from her expression even before she spoke. "We're gonna be in trouble if more of us get sick after this."

"Yeah, I know. Shit. Jacinda looked pale." Leo leaned back against a desk as Emma approached with two ginger ales.

"But I just figured she was just kept up by the case. Or that it was a twenty-four-hour bug or something small."

Emma passed one ginger ale to Leo and gestured to the men's room. Rather than giving the other to Denae, she offered her a little smile. "I got this."

"Oh, thank you. I owe you." Denae wilted against the wall by the restroom, meeting Leo's eyes as the sound of Jacinda retching carried through the door. "Looks like D.C. news was right about the wicked stomach virus running rampant through the city. They've been talking about the bug for a week, so I guess we should've known it would hit the team at some point."

"Let's just hope the rest of us stay well." Leo glanced over his shoulder, back to the empty conference room and their abandoned whiteboard. "Seems like it's up to you, me, Mia, and Emma to make these visits. Hopefully, we'll get this case solved before the virus takes us out too."

Vance cursed from the other side of the door, groaning loud enough that the discomfort couldn't be ignored.

On that note, Leo decided he'd pick up some preemptive vitamin C before they talked to anyone else. Better safe than sorry…assuming it wasn't too late for that.

18

Emma left Denae to concentrate on the driving as they approached D.C.'s Cathedral Heights neighborhood. Staring out the window of the Bureau vehicle, she barely noticed the fancy homes passing by. Frustration thrummed in her gut, and she jounced her leg against the passenger seat.

If only she could talk to her fellow agents about the little ghost girl she'd seen at the cemetery…and what the girl had said.

The lady wasn't bad. Trying to save. He wanted the lady to leave with him, too, but her ears don't hear.

Who were the man and woman the ghost had spoken of, and what did it all mean? Were the girl's words even related to the team's case, or would she have spoken the same things to any person who happened to be able to hear her?

Emma assumed the ghost's comment was related to her own concerns, but whether that conclusion was based on hope or truth, she wasn't sure.

For now, though, she took the girl's claims as a somewhat flimsy confirmation that their unsub was a woman, and seriously considered whether there could be two people working together.

But who's "he" in that case? We've only seen signs of one person on video.

And what the hell had the girl meant about the "she" of this scenario trying to save "him"? Save him from what? Emma ran her tongue along her teeth and bit down the impulse to spill everything to Denae and hope the woman would keep an open mind. Because none of this made sense.

How could beheading people, sledgehammering crypts, and stealing embalmed heads to rearrange body parts save anyone from anything?

Denae turned into their destination neighborhood, humming along to a pop song on the radio, as Emma fought back her impulse to share. She didn't know enough to be helpful, which meant keeping quiet was the wiser choice.

A violent shiver ran through her.

Denae offered an apologetic smile and turned the heat a notch higher.

The cold wasn't the problem, though, winter weather notwithstanding. The nerves standing on end against her neck were a result of the question that had haunted her ever since she'd seen the first head placed on the wrong body.

Could they be dealing with some type of dark occult practice? The media loved to run stories about that sort of conjecture, but the stories rarely ended up reflecting the truth.

Maybe Marigold would know something about it? But I can't discuss details of an investigation with her. Dammit. I guess that's what the internet's for, but do I really want to be the one googling "head swapping ritual murder?"

"It's just on the next block." Denae turned at a stop sign and slowed. "So I'm going to start looking for parking. Seems like none of these people have driveways big enough for their multiple cars."

Emma examined the car-lined street with Denae. They tried not to block the driveways of their interviewees when they could avoid it. Blocking in somebody's car always made an interview seem more threatening. Not much could be gained from scaring folks.

"What, all these people work from home? Sheesh." Denae kept muttering under her breath, finally parallel parking just a few addresses down from their destination.

Emma grabbed her bag and slipped out of the car in unison with Denae, heading down the sidewalk at a fast pace. The sky appeared ready to erupt with a storm, and Emma doubted the weather would hold off until lunch.

Plus, she wanted to get this interview underway and give her brain something else to stew on.

Something other than the little girl and the "they" who clearly hadn't forgotten about Emma like she'd hoped. Not when the girl had said "they" were there and that Emma needed to run.

I've got to talk to Marigold about this as soon as I get a chance. For potential answers and my own sanity. Maybe I can figure out a way to bring up the head swapping too.

Denae led the way up the sidewalk of a cookie-cutter home, white with red shutters and a mahogany door. Neat shrubs lined the walkway and the windows. The SUV in the drive was too clean for a D.C. winter, suggesting a recent wash.

"I think this couple cares about appearances." Emma rang the bell. "No matter what else we learn here."

A Black woman in blue hospital scrubs opened the door. She wore a tight smile, as if she could guess what Emma had been talking about. She ushered them in through their introductions and led them to an open-concept living area full of modern furniture.

Barb Royer barely let them sit down before she handed Emma a notepad with four women's names on it. Then she took a seat across from them. "These are the women I know of." She sat straighter, as if warding off the judgment that might come her way before she continued. "But I'm certain there are more."

Emma handed the list to Denae to review and gave what she hoped was a sympathetic smile.

The woman's tense face didn't return the smile, however. Instead, her eyes narrowed. "All due respect, I have to be at the hospital in a few hours, and I've got some errands to run prior to that. If we can get on with things? Rick and I had no children, and he did have affairs, but we made our marriage work. I have no idea where he was the night he was killed. What else do you need to know?"

I expected a grieving widow. This woman seems more pissed.

"Mrs. Royer," Emma leaned forward, "I am sorry for your loss, and we'll take up as little of your time as possible. If you could tell us a bit about how you knew of your husband's affairs, that might be a good place to start."

The woman sighed, a bit of the tension leaving her as she leaned back in her chair, lithe arms crossed over her chest. "Either of you married?"

For a moment Emma had the odd, sad urge to laugh. Marriage was so far outside her experience, Barb might as well have asked if she'd been to the moon. She'd lived alone so long that Emma almost couldn't comprehend knowing another person as intimately as Barb clearly knew Rick.

Emma shook her head along with Denae.

"Well, you're married long enough, you get to know when a person isn't being a hundred percent with you. And Rick isn't...*wasn't*...a good liar." Barb Royer paused there, frowning as she gestured to an award for most-valued employee hanging near the fireplace.

Emma squinted, making out Rick Royer's name in small print. "I understand."

Barb lifted a shoulder, like their discussion was no big deal. "We've both made priorities of our jobs, and that hurt our marriage. A while back, Rick needed to work nights more and more. There'd be sudden business meetings with international clients in different time zones." She scoffed. "Hell if I know why an office supply store manager would have business that urgent."

Emma's heart squeezed for the woman. "Did that happen often?"

The shoulder rose and fell again. "There'd be nights when he'd claim he needed to do inventory and might or might not end up sleeping at the office. He'd return at ungodly hours of the night and early morning, smelling like another woman."

Emma couldn't even imagine the feelings this woman would have dealt with through all that...her anger made sense. The seething expression on her face didn't come close to making her a suspect on its own, but Mrs. Royer's animosity also wasn't something they could overlook.

Especially considering how fast she'd reported her husband missing, and the valid reasons she had to be livid with him, assuming the list was accurate.

Denae sat forward on the couch, all business. "Mrs. Royer, you reported Rick missing a lot faster than the norm, considering he's an adult. Can you tell us about that?"

"You know, although Rick sometimes made it sound like he'd be sleeping at work, he almost always came home. And when he didn't, he called. Before our normal bedtime, or close to it anyway. Even if I was at work, he called to let me know. When he didn't call by midnight...well, call it a wife's intuition. Something felt off. So I called him."

She paused, her eyes glazing as her face softened just a touch.

"And when you called him...?" Denae prodded.

"When Rick didn't answer, and didn't call back within thirty minutes or so..." She shook herself, focusing back on the agents. "I knew something was wrong. And I was right."

Emma ran her fingers against each other. On the off chance that Barb Royer was their killer, they needed to gauge her reactions to certain hot-button questions, even if answers weren't forthcoming.

She caught the widow's eye and leaned forward. "Mrs. Royer, I'm sorry to have to ask this, but why would you stay with a man you were sure was so unfaithful to you?"

The smile that came to Barb Royer's face was so sad, a hint of relief ran through Emma's blood. A woman who smiled like that—with that level of resignation and jadedness touching her features—had long accepted whatever she was about to say. Something awfully serious would have had to happen to make this woman fly off the edge and change the status quo.

"I guess..." Her gaze wandered around the room, resting on shelves and end tables where little glass jars sat beside books, lamps, and coasters. She stared at the jars for a few seconds before coming back to Emma. "I just didn't want to lose my marriage. My comfort zone. In the beginning, I thought it was a sort of seven-year-itch thing, and Rick would come back to me. And then he didn't, but we were comfortable enough together. Satisfying jobs, good friends, nice neighborhood...I guess I stayed for the same reasons Rick never left."

Denae had pulled out her iPad and tapped in a few notes before taking up the conversation. "And there was nothing suspicious to worry about? Enemies, or maybe a woman who didn't like that he stayed with you instead of her?"

Barb shook her head. "Oh gosh, nothing like that. Nothing nearly so exciting. Not ever. I got those names from phone messages and emails. Common curiosity. I told myself I'd confront him someday, but…" She paused there, grimacing, and sat forward to gaze between Denae and Emma.

"The comfort zone can be seductive," Emma offered.

A smile played on the woman's lips. "Yes, so I just stayed there. Simple as that. Are those women capable of murder? I have no idea, but I felt it was my duty to hand the names over just in case. But I never saw any sign of an enemy or stalker or anything else that would've made me worry for him. Everyone always thought Rick was such a nice guy, and I suppose he was…"

"But…?" Emma prompted.

"You know, he would always treat spiders and bugs like they were people. He'd collect them in these little jam jars you see everywhere and just take them outside, saying, 'There you go, little buddy.'"

Barb's eyes filled with tears, and she dropped her chin, her chest heaving with sobs.

Emma shifted, coughing on the tension in the emotion-heavy air.

Denae pressed tissues into the woman's hand. "Can we get you some water?"

After a few deep breaths, Barb lifted her face to look at them again. Her eyes were red and moist. "I loved that man. He was just a damn cheat, but I loved him."

Denae followed up with a few further questions, while Emma used the facilities. Going around the corner to the half bath, she wondered if Rick's attachment to his home would encourage his ghost to appear and maybe offer vital information.

Yet, by the time she flushed the toilet and washed her hands—never having considered actually using the toilet, of course—she'd seen nothing. So she rejoined Denae and their interviewee back in the living room. Barb's mood had shifted. Her earlier sadness was gone, replaced by a mask of frustration or possibly rage.

Denae nodded as Emma sat back down. "And there's still no word about his car?"

"None." Barb sighed, frowning. "It's old enough that there's no tracking, and it's not here or at his work. I gave the police his laptop, in case they'd be able to get something from that, and I hear they've got access to his computer at the business, too, but…" She shrugged and went silent.

"That's all right." Denae tucked her iPad away. "We understand, and we're on the lookout. We'll let you know what we find. You've already helped quite a bit. That list of women is a good place for us to start." She stood, and Emma followed suit.

Barb Royer rose to escort them back to the door, walking slowly. Some of the air had been taken out of her, and Emma suspected she'd been ready to defend herself for putting up with the affairs. Now she was just an upset, grieving woman.

"I know it looks bad," Barb rested her hand against the doorframe, speaking low, "like I had reason to want my husband dead."

Emma stopped halfway out the door, exchanging a glance with Denae. "Mrs. Royer, that's not—"

"No, it's fine." The woman waved her off, her voice quavering for the first time since they'd arrived. "But there was something about Rick. You'd have to have met him. He was just too easy to love. I never could've hurt him…no matter how many times he destroyed me. I hate him for what he did, but I love him too."

Barb Royer swallowed hard, but the woman had a depth of resilience and strength that was impressive to witness. She lifted her chin and stood straighter.

"Barb, I'm so sorry." Denae squeezed the woman's arm. "It sounds like the two of you loved each other very much, even with Rick's affairs."

"He didn't deserve me. I know that." Barb's voice broke, but the certainty in her gaze held Emma frozen in the entryway. "But he didn't deserve to get his head chopped off by some nutjob either. And now I need you to find his killer if I'm ever to know another moment of peace in my life. So if there's anything else you need from me, you call."

Denae offered what further consolation she could, promising they'd be in touch.

Emma's words froze in her throat as she tried to breathe in the suddenly chilled air.

Ned Logan's ghost, with his see-through head, observed her from the front yard of the Royers' home.

She wondered if she'd ever know a moment of peace again.

19

Leo passed Mia a post-lunch cup of coffee as he sat down beside her at the conference table.

She was still viewing the final minutes of the Felicity Tree CCTV footage sent over by Detective Danielson. Leo'd escaped the last few boring minutes only by disposing of their to-go containers and grabbing some more caffeine. "I miss anything?"

She paused the video long enough to raise one perfectly shaped eyebrow at him before turning back to the laptop.

Right. Another exciting afternoon at the Bureau.

Saying the footage was "spotty at best," as Detective Danielson had told him earlier that day, was an understatement.

Leo sipped his coffee and stared at the screen with her. Dull as it was, they needed to at least make sure they viewed everything. Otherwise, it'd be just their luck to miss something relevant in the last few captured seconds.

So far, though, they'd gained nothing. No clear path for any of the victims. No suspicious activity or suggestion of new suspects. And no sign of Jay South's car leaving his bar's parking lot, because the man kept only one camera in operation, and it was aimed at the front door.

"There's still no sighting of the victims' cars?" Mia asked. "That's kind of key at this point."

Leo tapped his phone to double-check for missed messages, but only his wallpaper gazed back at him. No notifications. "Last message was from Emma, telling us they got a few names from Barb Royer but no information on her husband's car's whereabouts. The hunt's still on."

"By the sound of your voice, you don't think we're likely to find anything, do you?" Now that the video footage had come to a stop, Mia closed it out.

Leo frowned and ran one finger around the rim of his half-empty mug. "I don't think it's likely, no. Since the victims were led to a location with enough privacy to remove their heads, and since that crime scene still hasn't been found, I'm thinking their vehicles will be as hard to find as their bodies."

Mia pursed her lips like she wished she could disagree. Instead, she drank the last of her coffee and slammed down the cup, as if for emphasis. "You ready to tackle interviewing William Rigert's widow? That's next on our to-do list, right?"

"Let's do it." Leo finished his coffee, then grabbed his coat and bag for the ride.

In a fleet Ford Expedition, they reviewed what they knew of Rigert, the inhabitant of the third desecrated crypt.

Dead only nine months, following a sudden heart attack, Rigert had been in his early forties. No criminal background, and he'd been a longtime employee of a local foundry. Nothing suspicious or standout about the man, so far as the records suggested.

The apartment complex where he'd lived appeared as nondescript as the man himself. Leo parked in a lot with no markings to suggest where guests might park versus tenants.

They had to skirt trash as he and Mia headed toward the staircase to unit 209. He waved to a downstairs neighbor peering through her blinds, but she only scowled back at him before turning away.

"Friendly, huh?"

Mia chuckled. "We're law enforcement, and people can tell. Look around you. Run-down apartments in D.C., blinds mostly closed? Folks around here are gonna mind their own business."

Leo led the way up the rickety staircase to a balcony that fronted three units. He knocked on the door for unit 209. Inside, the volume on the TV lowered, and a forty-something woman with graying red hair and brown eyes appeared at the door.

World-worn, Jessa Rigert's expression matched her frayed bathrobe as she waved them in. She wore sweats underneath. Leo wondered whether the extra layer of French terry was more for comfort or for warmth.

"Thanks for speaking with us." Leo perched on a sofa in front of the television beside Mia. "And at such a difficult time. I'm sorry about what's happened to bring us here."

Jessa eyed him over the coffee table, which was littered with empty beer bottles and takeout containers. Dark circles bagged under her eyes, more prominent in the light beside the armchair she curled into. "I'm sorry about the mess. I don't have it in me to do much cleaning anymore."

Mia smiled gently, her expression full of sympathy. "Since this most recent problem, or…?"

"Since William died." Jessa Rigert pulled her feet in tighter beneath her, snuggling the robe around her like a blanket. "Nine months ago. I haven't been the same since. I don't…I don't know how people go on after they lose their soulmate. I can't even think straight anymore…"

Mia took the woman's hands and squeezed. "I'm so sorry for your loss."

Jessa clung to Mia's hand. "Every moment, everything I do or think, takes me back to our best times. To what we should have together in the future. Now I don't even feel like there *is* a future for me. I've been surviving off his insurance plan. He was a good, honest, hardworking man, and that's been a godsend…but I know that money won't last forever."

The hair on the back of Leo's neck sprang to life as he listened to this woman's despair. "There are resources that can help."

Jessa let Mia go and wiped her eyes. "I had to use so much of it to pay for the burial, but it's what we'd always talked about, lying together in death the way we had in life. I was supposed to be there with him when my time came."

"It's a terrible thing, but he'd want you to keep going and to be happy." From the look in the woman's eyes, she didn't believe him. Leo met Mia's gaze. It was time for a change of subject.

Concern radiated off Mia as she reviewed what they'd discovered of William's life, prompting nods from his widow.

Beside her, Leo's throat tightened at the tears drifting unchecked down Jessa's cheeks as she answered Mia's gentle questions. Too easily, the pain in her eyes reminded him of life after his parents died, and then again after his grandfather passed so suddenly.

Memory had been like a force of nature in those weeks, heavy and torturous. Not something he could forget.

"I answered all these questions nine months ago," Jessa shifted in her seat, her voice rising a little and bringing Leo back to focus on the conversation, "and there's nothing new to say! He wasn't on drugs. Never affiliated with any gang violence. Never accused of any crimes. He was just a great guy who made a good life for us despite the poverty we grew up in. There's no sense. No reason for what happened. His heart attack or…or this."

Jessa's eyes drifted toward a beer bottle that still held a quarter of its liquid, and Leo could practically feel the desperation emanating from her. Not even two in the afternoon, and she wasn't drunk, but she was numb…and she'd be passed out on her couch, insensible to the world, within a few hours of their leaving. The woman was attempting to drink away her pain, and just like with the life insurance money, only so much time could pass before that strategy became a real problem and she'd see her life further destroyed.

Leo leaned forward, willing his voice to remain steady. "And, forgive me for asking, but there were no enemies in William's life? He died from a heart attack, but—"

"No!" Jessa's eruption hung in the air, and Leo wouldn't have been surprised if the sound carried through the walls of the little apartment. "No enemies, okay? He wasn't a fucking gangster. He was just my husband. There was no reason for this!"

Sobs broke out of her throat, and she curled deeper into her armchair.

Mia glanced at him helplessly, shrugging.

"I'm sorry, Mrs. Rigert," Leo announced and pushed to his feet. "We'll leave you to…to your grief. And we'll be in touch with news when we can. There are answers out there, and we're going to find them. I promise."

The woman shrugged, lifting one arm to wave them away without looking back.

Leo opened the door for Mia and shut it behind them.

"She's right, in a way." Leo gripped the banister, slick with rain. "But also wrong. The individual who did this had reasons that made sense to them."

Mia muttered her agreement as she walked ahead of him down the stairs.

He swallowed down frustration, focusing on making sure he didn't slip. William Rigert's death had taken everything from the woman they'd just spoken to, and this added desecration of his crypt was all the more of an injustice, mocking the happy life she'd had. Her *soulmate*, she'd called the man. Not a word anyone spoke lightly once they reached middle age.

Whatever psychopathic code is involved, whatever's going on, we're going to figure it out. For her and everyone else being affected by this mess.

Mia swung into the passenger seat and rubbed her hands together, turning on the heat as soon as the engine started. "Jessa's description of William pretty much matches Janet Schmidt's description of her ex, Terry Derby. To the proverbial T. Not only did both men not have enemies, but they also seemed to be exceedingly nice guys."

"And Emma said Barb Royer said her husband was generally a great guy except for being a cheater." Leo pulled out of the apartment complex, eyeing the sky and wondering if there'd be more rain still. "Add that to an ex-wife saying the same…seems like there's a pattern there, but I don't know how we reconcile that with Sid Waller's convict status and what we've heard about Jay South."

Mia hummed in agreement. "Two extraordinarily kind people…three if we discount Rick Royer's cheating…plus one criminal, and one bartender somewhere in the middle of the spectrum. Hard to see a pattern when you put all of them together, I agree."

"Emma and Denae should be on their way to interview Marcus Peabody's family by now." Leo glanced at his phone, checking for notifications again. News was scarce and coming in rarely on this case so far. "We'll soon be able to compare notes on him and get the full rundown on what Rick Royer's wife said. See if any similarities become clearer then."

Focusing on the drive back to the Bureau, Leo let things rest there and left Mia to check in on Vance and Jacinda via text. There didn't seem to be much point in continuing on that train of thought right now anyway. The social reputations of their victims might be nothing more than a coincidence, or even a matter of two women who didn't want to speak ill of the dead.

Jessa had displayed real grief, but he hadn't seen the widows of Terry Derby or Rick Royer up close. While he trusted his colleagues...well, the urge to make someone out to be a hero after death was a real phenomenon he'd seen more than once. With that in mind, comparing likability cards could prove a total waste of brainpower as far as the victim profiles went.

And despite his earlier certainty that there had to be a method to this killer's madness...what if there wasn't?

We're downriver of a shitstorm of confusion coming our way, that's what.

20

Denae pulled to a stop in front of a ramshackle house. The Peabody home was one of a long row of shotgun-style houses lined up on a hill. Most of the structures were just a few heavy gusts from needing serious repair. This one was offset by peeling white paint, shutters that might once have been considered green, and a porch with sagging rails.

As Emma stepped out onto the curb, the curtains on the house to the left were yanked closed, and a few houses down, a woman hurried her steps toward her own front porch. This wasn't a neighborhood where folks talked to federal agents—though they did recognize their presence when Feds came calling.

"No more welcome than we are trusted." Denae's muttered comment carried them up toward the front door, which was just opening to greet them.

Amanda Peabody's brown hair had been pulled back tight. Her red-rimmed gray eyes were puffy from crying. A soaked tissue in her hand suggested her tears had been ongoing. "Thank you for coming."

She stepped back and waved them inside and down the

central hallway toward the kitchen. The house was warm and neat, though in disrepair, and Emma took a seat beside Denae in the kitchen, both of them easing down across from Amanda Peabody. Nearby, a tall teenager stood washing dishes at the sink, but he barely acknowledged them.

"That's my son Christopher. His brother'll be along soon." The woman's comment ended in a sob, and the boy at the sink flinched, as if the sound of his mother's pain hurt him.

Emma's heart clenched at the sight of the boy's reaction… this was a close family, and one in pain. "Mrs. Peabody, I'm so sorry we have to intrude. I'm sorry about…everything. But we're trying to find answers for you and your sons. Perhaps we could start by you telling us about your husband and his death?"

The woman tugged more tissues from a box at the center of the table just as a younger boy came in the back door, stomping his feet on a mat to rid his boots of mud. Emma remembered from their records that he was twelve. Though, looking at him, she noted the frown on his face added a few years. Mrs. Peabody gestured him over to sit beside her so she could wrap her arm around his shoulders.

"This is my youngest, Jacob. He and his brother take good care of me," she offered a pinched smile, "now that Marcus is gone. Seems like yesterday, but it's been six years. That was hard enough, but the idea of someone robbing a poor man's crypt, breaking into his casket…"

When the room went silent again, Denae leaned forward, resting her hands on the table. "We are going to do our best to find you answers, ma'am. We'd appreciate anything you can tell us."

Mrs. Peabody squeezed her youngest's shoulder for support. "Right, of course. That's why you're here. Marcus was a good, kind man. Always found a way to look at the bright side of life, even when others couldn't. He was the unfortunate victim of a gang-related drive-by shooting. Not the target of anyone, you understand, but he took a bullet from that gun, and that was his end."

Emma traded glances with Denae. "And you're sure he wasn't—"

"He wasn't the target." Soft-voiced but firm, Christopher Peabody held Emma's eyes. Respectful of who she was, the teen was still willing to step up to his father's defense while also keeping his cool.

Impressive. Amanda might look weak, but she'd raised strong, smart boys.

"Not arguing," Emma assured them. "I promise. We're just learning what we can."

Mrs. Peabody gestured for her oldest child to sit at the head of the table. When he'd relaxed into the chair, she refocused on Denae and Emma. "Marcus had absolutely nothing to do with that shooting. He certainly didn't deserve to die in such a way. And he didn't deserve to have his remains treated with such disrespect six years later."

Denae took a deep breath, then spoke in a gentle tone. "Mrs. Peabody, if you don't mind me asking…crypts in mausoleums are expensive. And please understand I don't mean any offense, but—"

"No, no, I get it," the woman huffed a laugh, seeming to relax for the first time since they'd entered, "you see our house and wonder how we afforded it. Thing is, Marcus wasn't close to his parents. We married young, and he was slow to reconcile with them over not living up to *their expectations*. When he died, his parents swept in and took care of all the costs. A sort of apology that came too late. They still send me money, sometimes, to help with the boys."

In the background, a white-eyed old woman peered in through the back door—focused on Amanda and her sons, not the agents—and nodded and moved on, seeming to have contented herself that they weren't being harassed. Emma wondered what the old woman would have done if she and Denae had been there to question suspects rather than victims. Anything?

Maybe I should get up. Follow her and see what she can tell me...

But the moment was gone, and realistically, Emma didn't believe the woman would give her the time of day.

She'd just been glancing in on a neighbor, still a concerned member of the community.

Or avoiding Emma, maybe.

Emma shook herself back to the moment, with Amanda talking about how Marcus had helped raise funds for a local basketball league for the boys and their peers, then served as a coach. There was no denying the fact that he sounded like he'd been a good man, and a wonderful father.

Amanda stumbled to a halt, her boys supporting her on each side, and Emma leaned forward and took one of her hands. "Mrs. Peabody, I promise we'll get to the bottom of this. We're investigating a number of avenues and should have more information in the next forty-eight hours or so. We'll be in touch when we do."

Christopher frowned and met his brother's eyes before turning back to the agents. "Dad'll be dead no matter what you find, but it'd be good to know."

Another sob slipped from his mother's lips. "Chris is right. I guess it doesn't matter, but we need to make sure Marcus is laid to rest again."

The unspoken implication hung in the air...they needed to make sure *all of him* was laid to rest again. Head and body.

Standing with Denae, Emma led the way toward the front of the house, with Christopher trailing behind to open the door. He thanked them for their time, playing the man of the house well for a fourteen-year-old, and Emma did her best to shut the door fast. The young man turned the lock behind them.

On the way back to the car, though, she couldn't help thinking about what Christopher Peabody had said. Yes, their father would still be gone, no matter what the investigation uncovered. He'd still be gone from their lives.

But that didn't necessarily mean he'd gone very far.

21

As the couch caught me like a hammock, for a moment, I thought the solid furniture swayed beneath me. The fatigue talking, almost definitely.

Disposing of Rick Royer's body in the lake had been even harder than taking care of Terry Derby. The second man had been a little heavier, and my muscles were in revolt after three solid days of hacking and sawing and lifting. Fighting me on every step, aching to lie down and sleep.

I rested my head against the back of the couch, closing my eyes for a temporary breather—just a few seconds, I promised myself—and spoke to Michael to keep myself from passing out completely.

He was always nearby now, making sure I remained alert and aware for him.

"Rick wasn't as nice a person as he seemed on the internet. Something about him felt…dirty." The observation hung between us. I opened my eyes to see Michael nodding, perched across from me on the coffee table. "I see from your face that you didn't like the man at all. But I hope he's still good enough for the soul renewal."

The air was too still. I felt myself drifting, every one of my muscles heavy and begging for sleep. Yet…I couldn't do that to Michael.

I pushed myself up to a sitting position, bracing my hands on my knees and leaning forward to focus on my husband. "I'm just so tired. But I'm awake, baby."

Michael frowned. "I'm tired of being a ghost. You have to keep going, Renata."

If only I could hug you. Touch you. This would be so much easier.

"Tonight's the third and final step." I didn't know whether the words were meant to comfort me or Michael more, but they lifted his head a touch. "Body renewal."

Stopping there, I heaved myself to my feet and headed to the kitchen. I didn't need to start warming up my next lasagna yet, but I needed something to eat. Fuel.

The exhaustion from all this physical exertion was unreal. Even though I'd trained and practiced, I supposed there was no real way to understand the effort involved in bringing back the dead until one did it.

I pulled out bread and lunch meat. The bread was stale, and the lunch meat had passed its best-by date, but beggars couldn't be choosers.

Bringing a loved one back from the dead doesn't leave much time for shopping, does it?

The thought made me laugh, but one glance at Michael told me he was less than amused. A scowl on his face proved that much. He'd gotten pushier and pushier since we'd started our three-day stretch, but at least he was speaking a bit more.

I still hesitated to tell him what I was worried about for later that night, though. He'd reprimand me for not having enough faith. But I had faith…as well as concerns. The lasagna and the dinner and the head removal would go off fine, but every time I thought about the security at Michael's cemetery, I wanted to scream.

To restore his body and finish the renewal ritual, I had to break into Michael's crypt and take his head. The problem was, how was I supposed to get past the security at Cedar Grove Cemetery? When I'd interred Michael, I'd selected the best. Initially, it'd seemed the responsible thing, selecting a well-maintained location for his eternal rest.

It wouldn't just be the mausoleum and crypt that were locked, though, but also the graveyard, with tall, secure fencing lined with cameras that I'd somehow have to avoid. I had done my due diligence and examined the fence on several occasions over the past three years. I knew where I would need to go to break in safely. But it wouldn't be easy.

This night's chore was going to require more strength and determination compared to the last two nights. My whole body ached with the desire to go rest in my bed and sleep for days.

Swallowing down exhausted tears, I stumbled to the kitchen table and stared at the little plate I'd made for myself. An unappetizing sandwich, chips, and a few pickles. The plate looked like sadness manifested. "I miss your cooking, Michael."

The whisper hung between us. Michael came closer and stood by the table. His presence offered more confidence and energy than the calories in front of me, but I started eating anyway. The food tasted of nothing. Texture and pressure on my tongue were the only evidence I was eating at all.

"I don't know if I can do this."

"I know you're worried. I know." He crouched beside me, observing me with those sweet blue eyes. "But you'll figure tonight out. I know you can do it, and I'll be there with you every step of the way."

Swallowing a stale lump of bread, forcing the dry food

down my throat, I tried to straighten in my seat. To not show Michael how bone-tired exhausted I was.

He deserves the best from me. He does. I have to keep going.

"I know, babe." I picked up a pickle, willing the crunch and the acidic sting against my lips to wake me up. "But maybe I should take a quick nap—"

"No! Renata, you promised me!"

His cry tore through my heart, just about bursting my nerves.

He stood and rounded the table to sit across from me, staring into me with those wide blue eyes, so full of hurt.

I can do this.

"I'm sorry." I pushed my unfinished meal away and stood, facing him across our little kitchen. "Forgive me, babe. I'm sorry."

He frowned, brow creased and tight. He eventually retreated to the living room to sulk. I knew he'd be with me again later. This process was tough on both of us.

I wasn't imagining it…Michael really had grown more demanding since his death. I assumed dying had to be horribly stressful, but I still wished he could give me some ideas for the night's venture. A brainstorming session would help me focus and boost my confidence.

When I needed ideas more than ever, he remained silent. He'd done this before. He observed me coldly from the next room as I forced myself to finish eating, taking in some nutrients before moving on to the next task. Even as he kept me to my promise to remain awake with him for these three days.

Three days. We're in this together.

"We're close, Renata." His voice echoed through the home. "So close. You just have to carry the ritual through. I don't want to leave you forever. Don't give up on me. Omne trium perfectum. Remember, please."

The despair in his voice drove me over to the doorway into the main room, where I glimpsed him drifting near the door.

That he felt he needed to ask me not to give up on him…

"I won't, love." I choked back a sob, ignoring the leaden feel in my feet and limbs. "I'll never give up on you."

The coffee maker beeped, and I turned back to pour myself a tall cup, my fourth or fifth today. I'd had so many I was losing count. But it didn't matter.

"Spirit, soul, body. Spirit, soul, body. Spirit, soul, body." The chant centered me, just like always.

There was work to be done. Armed with a heavy dose of caffeine, I'd run my errand, then I'd work on the lasagna. I had to. Time was short.

22

Leo flashed his credentials to the representative at the central kiosk in the Bank of the Potomac—where one of Rick Royer's affairs worked. "We're looking for Carol Jackson. Is she in today?"

The representative's eyes narrowed. Lines of concern appeared across her forehead. "Can I ask what this is about? Carol's working right now."

Beside him, Mia's toe tapped the shiny marble flooring. She turned toward the line of tellers, probably already thinking they should be allowed to bypass the main desk.

Leo forced a smile to his lips, keeping his voice low, even though no customers stood nearby. "Yes, I realize she'd be working right now, but we do need to speak with her. We wouldn't be here if it weren't important."

For a second, he thought the woman might argue with him, but instead she walked over to the bank of tellers. She pulled aside a middle-aged woman with long brown hair and held a fast, whispered conversation.

Mia leaned closer to him. "You see how her face just went white? That's a woman who's not pleased to see us."

"And one with long brown hair too." Leo went quiet as Carol Jackson approached, walking quickly, considering how tall her heels were.

"Agents, I'm told you need to see me, but I'm at work and—"

"We wouldn't be here if it weren't important, Ms. Jackson." Mia gestured to the offices beside them, all occupied. "It looks pretty busy here. Is there a place we can talk?"

Carol hesitated, but the first woman gestured toward a hall leading off from the back of the open lobby. She sighed. "This way."

Following Carol into the back, Leo couldn't help thinking that she was acting awfully skittish for someone who'd done nothing more than have an affair. Her stride was fast and long, as if she were considering an escape.

They passed offices with brass nameplates indicating *Branch Manager* and *Chief Loan Officer*. When she came to an unmarked door on their left, she ushered them into an empty office with nothing more than a desk and a few chairs. Waiting for a new employee, Leo supposed.

Carol sat behind the desk and indicated they should sit in the other chairs. "I need this job, Agent Ambrose, Agent Logan, and you're making a scene in my workplace. I need you to be quick and explain why you're here. Everyone's skittish about the Feds. A security guard was arrested a few weeks ago for robbing another bank."

That explained quite a bit. Leo perched on one of the velvet chairs. "This has nothing to do with robbery. We'll try to be quick, Ms. Jackson. We're attempting to find out who killed a man we believe you had a relationship with on some level."

Licking her lips, the woman tapped one heel against the wall at her back, anxiety radiating off her more than her floral perfume. "Rick." She raised one hand to her eyes and shook her head. "I don't know anything about what happened. Just what I heard on the news, that is...enough to be scared. And Rick was..."

"Take your time." Mia's voice was soft, but Leo knew her well enough to read the frustration. Talking to Carol was amounting to pulling teeth. Mia flashed a gentle, dimpled smile to try to take the edge off Carol's anxiety...hopefully encouraging her to speak openly.

A pained laugh escaped the woman, and for a second, Leo thought she'd break into sobs, but her eyes were dry when she regained focus.

"I'm sorry. I've just got little to say. Rick was important to me. This is...hard. I guess I knew you'd show up with questions, but I've been trying not to think about him ever since I heard...heard..."

"We understand." Mia leaned forward. "But if you could tell us about your relationship, how you met, and what Rick was like, we'd appreciate it. You never know what might help an investigation in a case like this."

Carol swallowed hard before she glanced between Leo and Mia and began talking. "I knew Rick was married from the first time we messed around. He banked here, and his wife's name was on the account, for crying out loud."

"We're not here to judge," Leo said.

"Yeah, I know. His marriage was never a secret. And I never meant to get involved with a married man...but Rick was so charming. So kind. We spent a lot of time together in hotels, and I grew very attached to him. Until he told me that he 'just can't do this anymore.' Those were his exact words. And it wasn't that he was trying to work things out with his wife either. He told me that was what was going on, but I knew that was a lie just from the expression on his face. Like he was swallowing unchewed taffy down when he said it."

Carol shook her head and began pulling her long hair out

of the bun at her neck, twisting the strands apart and back together. A nervous habit, maybe.

Mia leaned toward her. "I'm sorry to have to ask this. Had he found someone else? We understand Rick had multiple affairs—"

"Ha." Carol sat back in her chair, shaking her head. With her hair up, her cheekbones had been more prominent, but as her hair fell around her face, her edges softened. She'd taken a decade off with the change in style, and no longer appeared so haggard or spooked as she had a few moments before. "You could say that, I guess. I followed him one night after he got off work. Thinking he was probably infatuated with someone new, and I just had to see her. See if she was so much younger or prettier than me."

Mia took a pack of tissues from within her coat as a few tears started leaking from Carol's eyes. The bank teller lifted one to her face, pursing her lips as if Mia's gesture had made it harder for her not to begin crying outright.

Impatience amping up his nerves, Leo bounced his toe against the desk a smidge too loudly, drawing the interviewee's attention back to him. "And you found...what? Where did following him take you?"

"He was just spending his evening at a strip club. Maybe falling for a stripper or maybe just bored with me. Either way, his ghosting me broke my heart." A choked sob left her throat as she swiped at her eyes with the tissues. "I thought he was going to leave his wife for me. Eventually."

If he hadn't been presented with the claim so often, Leo wouldn't have been able to keep a straight face. Why did people having affairs always think that?

Man or woman, they always seemed to believe that the person who was outright lying to their spouse, being unfaithful on the regular, would turn around and offer them nothing but the truth. True love and all that. The pattern was as painful as it was absurd.

"Were there any hard feelings after that?" Leo leaned forward from his perch, resting his elbows on his knees and speaking low. "Any grudges?"

Carol glanced out the window at her side, frowning. "I should've seen it coming. Rick was just…being Rick."

At least she recognized that. *Might keep her from making the same mistake twice. Maybe.*

"You said you were heartbroken. So did you tell anyone close to you about how things ended? How he moved on from your relationship?"

"Oh, no!" Carol sat up straighter and stared at them, eyes wide. "Absolutely no one. You have to understand…my family is very religious. So are most of my friends. Even here…"

She gazed at the door, her lips pursed. The tears she'd been fighting back had dried, but she'd gone pale.

Leo held in a sigh. "You didn't even tell your colleagues, you mean?"

"I couldn't tell anyone." She focused back on Mia, then Leo. "Please, you have to do the same. You don't know what it could do to me if news of the affair came out. And him being a customer here."

Mia glanced over at Leo. Uncomfortable. Some secrets couldn't be guaranteed. She was thinking what he was thinking.

"We'll do our best to keep your history with Rick quiet." Leo allowed that to sink in before continuing. "But, Ms. Jackson, you have to understand this is an ongoing investigation, and details may come to light. We have to prioritize justice for Rick's murder, not any secrets the two of you may have kept while he was alive."

Carol opened her mouth, as if to protest, but ended up

only clenching her hands against her skirt and nodding. "I understand. Whatever you can do, I appreciate it."

Mia asked about the timing of the affair and hotels they'd visited, noting down various details that might or might not be of use later.

Carol Jackson ticked a lot of boxes. Caucasian. Brunette. Had an affair. Followed her lover.

"He wasn't the most romantic," Carol rubbed her hands together, "but he was a good man. To me. While we were together, I mean. And then, well…things changed. We had to move on. That's life, right?" She glanced up at them, seeming to realize what she'd just said. Rick was dead. There'd been no moving on for him. "I'm sorry, I shouldn't have said that." She shifted, twisting her hair. "But I don't know what else to tell you."

Leo stood from the desk, zipping his coat in preparation for the colder air outside. They weren't going to gain anything more from Carol Jackson right now. "We may have more questions for you. You're not a suspect," he lied as he handed her one of his business cards, "but please don't leave town without letting us know first."

Carol went a little green, her cheeks drawn, but she met his eyes and nodded.

He turned and followed Mia out into the hallway.

Once they arrived in the lobby, he paused long enough to note that Carol hadn't followed them out of the office yet. Naturally, she was shaken after talking about her dead lover…but a murderer could be just as shaken as a jilted lover.

Mia held the door open for him as they exited, and he spoke in a low voice to make sure the wind wouldn't carry his thoughts back inside as he shared his suspicions, including about how Carol fit the profile.

She paused, grimacing. "I was thinking the same thing."

Well, that's the two of us on the same page.

Leo opened the door of the Ford, cringing at a burst of cold wind that hit him from the side. "Any thoughts on visiting the nearest drive-through for some fresh coffee?"

Mia grinned. "Hurry up and get to driving."

23

Emma eyed the broken window running alongside the exterior door of the Luster Neighborhood Apartment Complex, building two. Cinnamon Lafayette, one of Rick Royer's many lovers, appeared to live a bit on the wild side. This complex didn't seem particularly welcoming to outsiders. "Guess someone was in a hurry, huh?"

Finding the handle unlocked, Denae held the door open for Emma. Denae followed her inside as she unzipped her coat. "Wonder if they even lock up at night anymore? Seems like the kind of place where you'd want 'em to, but..." She gestured back at the window.

Emma turned. *Enough said.*

They climbed the narrow staircase toward the third floor. There was nothing lustrous about the Luster Neighborhood Apartment Complex. The halls smelled of thousands of takeout dinners and millions of cigarettes. The inhabitants' lifestyles soaked into the wallpaper peeling from every vertical surface. At least the stairwell rails were metal...she wouldn't have trusted wooden ones in a disintegrating building like this one.

"I can't believe she legally changed her name to Cinnamon." Denae huffed as they reached the third floor. "Honestly, I don't know whether to be impressed or horrified. I don't know what that says about me."

Denae waved Emma farther down the hall, to the very end. Cinnamon Lafayette lived in unit 320, as far from the stairs as a tenant could get.

When Emma knocked, she almost expected the wrong person to answer. According to records, their interviewee was supposed to be on disability. That three-story climb had been a steep one.

Despite expectations to the contrary, the woman who came to the door matched the Facebook pictures they'd seen, with big curly hair and doe-like brown eyes.

She also leaned on a cane decorated with sparkles and was surrounded by a cloud of smoke.

"Cinnamon Lafayette?" Denae flashed her ID. "I'm Special Agent Denae Monroe, and this is my partner, Special Agent Emma Last. We're here to talk to you about a Rick Royer."

The woman sighed, leaning heavier on her cane, and glanced between them as she took one long drag on a nearly finished cigarette.

Emma tried for her friendliest smile. "I think one of our colleagues told you we'd be coming by?"

"Yeah." The woman took an awkward step backward and waved them inside. "Take a seat on the couch, but don't touch the cat. He bites."

Stepping forward into a dimly lit, smoky apartment, Emma wished she had a mask to cover her nose. Cigarette smoke warred with the incense rising from cluttered bookcases. Overstuffed furniture soaked up the smells, emanating the odor back into the air. Her eyes watered, but she moved past the smoke near the doorway and took a seat on the couch, sitting a good foot away from a lanky, mangy black feline lounging on one arm.

Denae perched beside her, placing Emma between the cat and herself. *Oh, sure, throw me to the lion.*

"I don't know how you maneuver up and down those stairs out there." Denae gestured to the sparkly cane as Cinnamon took a seat across from them. "They're about as brutal as a three-story climb could be."

"Man alive, I'd never make it up those." Cinnamon laughed. "You can't see it from the front, but the laundry room right next door has an elevator accessible for freight and anyone who needs it. Like me. Work accident," she patted her knee, "ended my career. I'm just lucky I'm so close to the elevator."

"It was a work-related injury?" Emma activated her iPad, preparing to take down notes. "I thought you worked at that strip club off the highway? Swinging Sweethearts, I think it's called? I guess I think of that work as being high risk in a different fashion."

Cinnamon sat back in her seat and killed the end of her cigarette in a nearby ashtray. "Yeah, I get it. But if you're upside down on a pole when a drunk asshole grabs your leg and tries to give you a spin-around, shit happens."

Denae's eyes went wide. "Seriously?"

Cinnamon tapped her knee. "Yep. By the time Billy, our bouncer, got there, I was in more pain than a mama giving birth to triplets. Knee's gone now. So's my career. Way the cookie crumbles and all that, right? I make do. And I've got things to do. Today."

The remark was pointed. Small talk would not make this woman open up any more than straightforward questioning would, so they might as well get on with it.

"I understand." Denae shifted on the couch, setting her coat carefully across her lap...to avoid having it soak up smoke from the couch, Emma guessed. "We won't take up more of your time than we need to. I know you've been told Rick Royer is dead. Authorities have every reason to believe it was a homicide, and we understand you were a known acquaintance of Rick's. We just need to know whatever you can tell us about him, your relationship...anything that might help us find his killer."

"Well, I sure as hell didn't do it." Cinnamon pushed some curls back from her face and gave a rueful laugh. "Guess my cane puts me a little ways down your suspect list, huh? Knee injury might be good for something, after all."

A chuckle escaped Emma's chest, bringing a more honest smile to Cinnamon's face.

"Look, things between me and Ricky ended fast. I never had real feelings for him and was never under the impression he had them for me. What we had was more like...a business relationship."

Emma typed as she spoke, trying to ignore the smoke in the air, which made for an oily slickness that seeped into her mouth every time she opened it. "Sounds like the two of you got along well. What ended things between you?"

"One day he was there...the next he wasn't. Just stopped coming to the club. Like I said, it was business between us. And I wasn't hurting for clients."

"How long ago was this?"

"About two months before that drunk asshole pulled me off the pole and ended my career."

The cat on the end of the couch straightened and stretched, meowing at Emma. She shifted toward Denae. Cinnamon said something in French, and the cat hopped down and went over to rub against her leg. "Guy Fawkes doesn't bite me, but he's not a fan of strangers." She scratched his chin. "Hey, my guard kitty. Good boy."

Good boy or not, I'm glad he's over there now instead of eyeing me.

"And did Rick ever get into any fights or altercations at the club," Denae pressed forward, her eyes also on the revolutionarily named black cat, "or anywhere else that you witnessed?"

"Ha." Cinnamon cupped her hands under the feline's belly and lifted him onto her lap, where he sat primly and surveilled the agents. "Ricky wasn't like Guy here. He was a lover, not a fighter. But…I mean…he was a coward. Couldn't even stand up to his wife. He was a super nice guy."

How many times were they going to hear that?

"Nice how?"

"Easy to get along with. Buddies with everyone as far as I saw. Didn't even talk dirt about his wife like most of my other regulars. Just seemed to want…more. And wasn't strong enough to go get it for himself. Like 'most everybody else on the face of the planet, I guess."

Emma caught Cinnamon's eyes directly. "You never mentioned knowing he had a wife, so why would you have expected him to 'talk dirt' about her?"

Cinnamon frowned. "I mean, I guessed he did. You gotta understand, though…even the guys who weren't married had some girl or woman they'd be complaining about. Ricky never did. The way to be sure a guy didn't have anyone was if he boasted about his woman all the time. The rare ones who stayed quiet and were nice, not dangerous…like Ricky… seemed to be taken, for sure. Even if they weren't happy."

"Fair enough." Emma popped a piece of gum into her mouth, hoping the spearmint would keep the smell of smoke at bay. She offered a piece to both women. Cinnamon declined. Denae practically tore the pack out of Emma's hand. "And so, I'm assuming you never met his wife? Or anyone you suspected of being with him?"

Cinnamon shook her head. "Sometimes, I worried she'd show up at the club. I know I'd sure as hell take a bitch out if they were screwing around with my man, 'specially one as nice as Ricky. But she never came around that I saw. Must've known about his extracurricular activities, though. He was at the club way too many nights for any sane spouse not to catch on."

She stroked her cat, scratching him under the chin until he purred. Watching her, Emma thought of Barb Royer, Rick's widow. The women couldn't have been more different from each other, but Rick had been attracted to both.

Denae asked a few more questions, trying to ascertain if Cinnamon had met any of the other victims. But on presentation of Terry Derby's photo and all the other pictures of the victims, Cinnamon just shook her head.

More and more, Emma worried that none of Rick's women would pan out. None of them seemed to have a connection to any of the other victims.

Denae's voice got somewhat hoarse as she continued questioning Cinnamon. Emma suspected her colleague was suffering the effects of the secondhand smoke just as much as she was.

Her throat felt clogged, despite the minty gum. And it didn't seem as if they had much more to gather. Her cat would have been more capable of creeping into the graveyard and causing bodily harm than the disabled woman seated across from them.

"We may have more questions." Emma stood up, willing herself not to cough 'til she reached the hall. "If we do, we'll call. Thank you for your time. And I hope your knee recovers."

Cinnamon hacked as a response—a longtime smoker's cough—and followed them to the door, thanking Emma for the well-wishes. Her cat followed on her heels, which Emma didn't miss. "By the way, how was Ricky killed?"

Denae paused with her hand on the doorframe, eyes squinted in discomfort. "That's not yet public information, Ms. Lafayette. Sorry."

Emma stepped out into the hall and slipped a card from her coat pocket. "If you think of anything, whether you think it's important or not, please call us."

Cinnamon's lips quirked, and her curls bobbled as she shook her head. "Wasn't nothing important about Ricky." And then she closed the door.

Denae sighed. "That's the problem, isn't it? There wasn't anything 'important' about any of these men."

"Except for being nice." Emma took a deep breath of the relatively fresh hallway air, heading back toward the staircase.

Emma's phone buzzed with an incoming call, and she tugged the device from her pocket to see Jacinda's smiling face gazing back. She held up a finger to pause Denae at the top of the staircase and took the call. "You've got me, Jacinda, and Denae's right beside me."

"Good. Don't put me on speaker, though. You can share the word with Denae once the two of you have some privacy. I got a call from Detective Danielson." The woman paused, and gagging could be heard through the line before she came back on. "Sorry. I need you two to head over to Holmes Park. Three severed human heads were just found there by a pair of joggers. They were left in gift bags."

Emma fought the urge to picture what that must've looked like, but she'd see soon enough.

"Complete," Jacinda coughed roughly, "with curly bows, if you can believe it. It's too soon for official confirmation that these are the missing heads, but—"

"But, really, how many missing heads can there be in this

city?" Emma finished the sentence as SSA Hollingsworth lost to another round of coughing. "And we need to find out ASAP."

"Right." Jacinda sighed raggedly. "Head over to Holmes and take a look at the crime scene. Now."

24

Detective Stanley Danielson stubbed out his cigarette and stuffed the butt into a coat pocket as Emma and Denae reached him. The man was positively grim, as if he'd been henpecked by both media and corpses alike that day. Emma tried for a smile but couldn't quite summon one.

They were there to collect disembodied heads. Even the lush pines of Holmes Park couldn't change the ghoulishness of that task.

"Special Agent Last, Special Agent Monroe. Thank you for coming so quickly." The detective turned on his heel and led them on a trail that ran deep into the park. "I won't say it's good to see you, under these circumstances."

Emma had hoped for footprints along the trail, but as luck or design would have it, their head-dropper had chosen an asphalt jogging path. The upshot was they had an easy walk to their crime scene.

After a few more turns, Emma glimpsed a concrete bench along the side of the trail. Crime scene tape floated in the chilly early evening air. Behind the tape were three brightly colored gift bags...along with a few plastic-wrapped heads. A couple forensic techs hovered nearby, waiting for the go-ahead from the agents.

"Keeping them fresh?" Emma asked.

Danielson didn't answer her directly. "The joggers who found the bags didn't use their better judgment. They picked them up, looked inside, and dropped the *gifts* when they realized what they were. I don't know what the original positioning was." The detective stopped and sighed, staring beyond the tape at their crime scene where the gift bags sat askew.

Emma removed her leather gloves and pulled on some latex ones, then ducked under the tape with Denae right behind her. One gift bag sat on its side on the bench. The top half of a plastic-wrapped head was just visible from within. A wisp of brown hair escaped the wrap and fluttered in the breeze, as if to say hello.

Another bag was on the ground with a smaller wrapped head beside it. "Your techs take that head out or your joggers do it?"

Danielson had stayed outside the tape. He had a new, unlit cigarette in his mouth, but he took it out to answer. "Techs haven't touched anything yet. I wanted you to look first. That head toppled out when the joggers dropped the bag. Hard to tell through the plastic wrap, but I'm thinking that's Sid Waller's head since it's more…uh…"

"Shrunken? Decomposed? Horrifying?"

Denae crouched to examine the head in question. "Yeah, Waller…I think. The features are totally indistinct right now, sunken and malformed. He's been dead a long time."

Emma crouched beside Denae. "And I'm betting this half-opened gift is the top portion of William Rigert, based on the brown hair."

"And unless we've got an unfound disturbed body, that makes the third head Marcus Peabody's. All heads accounted for." Denae glanced over at Emma, who was still crouched by the head on the ground. "You think this means our killer's done?"

Emma shook her head as she stood straight, peering between the three bags. "Even if the embalmed heads are recognizable and prove to be the ones we're missing...this unsub has exhibited a lot of violence. Fast. I'd like to believe they're done, but..."

The detective grunted and snapped a lighter closed, taking a drag from his smoke before replying. "But life's not that easy."

"Right." Emma peered around the crime scene, keeping an eye out for ghosts more than anything, but only finding techs and law enforcement. "I can't believe we're looking at gift bags decorated with cartoon butterflies, of all things. Like it's a kid's birthday party."

Denae gestured to the one with three orange butterflies. "They're kind of creepy. Smiling like that. Insects don't smile."

Emma waved the techs over and let them get to work.

"We'll get dental records for the heads and see if we can make an official identification that way." Danielson stepped back a few feet and pulled on his cigarette.

Emma nearly gagged at the sight of it. She'd been around enough cigarette smoke to last a lifetime.

Danielson continued. "Save the widows and family members the trauma of IDing heads. If dental work fails, I guess we won't have any choice. We'll have to bring in Amanda Peabody and Jessa Rigert. We've got dental on Sid Waller already...one stroke of luck since I don't know who'd identify him right now."

"Least of all in the state he's in." Denae walked around the bench, viewing the scene from all angles. "Man was in a crypt for a half-century."

"I wonder if the gift bags are a sign of compassion or some kind of sarcastic jibe at the victims and law enforcement…" Emma cut herself off, distracted by a tech lifting a long strand of hair from the bench. She signaled to him to pause and leaned in closer. "Long and brown."

Denae let out a whistle. "Not uncommon, but that's a pattern."

Emma peered farther down the trail. "Where are our unlucky joggers?"

"I've got them down at the station, filling out reports." The detective frowned at the hair. "They're a couple. Man with short blond hair and a woman with curly red hair. That strand didn't come from them."

Emma watched a tech bag the hair as evidence before she turned back to Denae. "No way to know right now if it's a match to the hair found at Van Der Beek Cemetery, but the lab should be able to tell."

Don't get your hopes up, Emma girl. That hair could belong to anyone. A public park isn't exactly an isolated property.

The tech who'd been dusting for prints around the bags held up a hand, calling for their attention. "I got a print inside this bag."

"Seriously?" Relief hit Emma in a dizzying wave, and she mentally crossed her fingers that the print would break the case. "Well, it didn't come from the head."

The tech's eyes went a little wide, but Denae barked a laugh and clapped him on the shoulder. "Good work, friend. That's amazing news."

Even a partial print could potentially identify their unsub. Emma met Detective Danielson's eyes across the yellow tape between them. "And you said the joggers only lifted the bags and peered inside before dropping them, right?"

He nodded through a swirl of cigarette smoke. "That print could be a big deal."

Peering up at the trees, Emma searched around for any security cameras. Some of the city's parks were wired, but she couldn't remember which ones or how extensive that surveillance might be. When she couldn't find any metal catching the sunlight, she focused back on the detective. "Any security footage of use? It's been a while since I had a crime scene at this park."

"There's a camera at the entrance and a CCTV cam hung on the entrance to each trail. Nothing here around this bench, but we do have options. My officers are collecting the footage from park security now."

Denae slipped off her latex gloves, and Emma did the same, collecting both pairs in an empty evidence bag for disposal. "And you know the drill—"

"Right, you are," the detective confirmed, "and I'll have it sent over to the VCU immediately."

Emma pulled on her winter gloves and flexed her fingers, the cold already cutting into her blood after this brief time outside. "Our team will want to interview the joggers after they've completed their statements. If any witnesses come forward, we'll speak to them as well."

After another quick look around, Emma led the way back toward the parking lot, calling Jacinda as they went. With the update finished, Jacinda told her she wanted the team back at the VCU office, where they could phone conference her in.

Denae unlocked the SUV, and both women hurried to get in and slam their doors on the cold air. The heater was blowing even before Emma could reel in a cold breath to reply.

"Jacinda sounds rough." Emma rubbed her cheeks, bringing feeling back. "And Mia's last text suggested Vance is even worse off."

Denae turned up the heater and pulled out of the parking spot, going a touch too slow for Emma's taste. "Well, we'll just have to rub it in their noses when we solve the case without them, huh?"

Chuckling, Emma agreed. Although her eyes remained on the edges of the park as they drove away, searching for any ghosts. She wasn't all that bothered to see not a single white-eyed gaze looking back at her.

Ghosts or not, they finally had real evidence, and a real chance of cracking the case wide open.

25

Leo set up the speaker in the conference room so Jacinda could easily address all of them...without being on screen. Their SSA sounded like absolute hell, and he imagined she looked it as well.

Meanwhile, Vance was too violently ill to conference in, so they were still down one agent for this roundup.

But they'd finally achieved real progress. He couldn't help smiling as Emma updated the whiteboard. The epic discovery of the missing heads and the results of the afternoon's interviews filled in the cracks on the murder board. He gave a silent clap when Emma pointed to the fingerprint and hair notations. Evidence meant they were getting somewhere.

"Everyone ready and present?" Jacinda's voice was hoarse, deep, and almost unrecognizable, but she sounded steady enough. That was something.

"All but Vance," Mia acknowledged.

"Okay, then." Jacinda coughed. "Let's get started. The toxicologist has expedited the victims' drug tests at the Bureau's request, but it'll still be at least two days before we get results. The most important finding they're working with is the fingerprint, which is being analyzed as we speak. The hair could also prove helpful in connecting the crime scenes, even if it won't give us a firm ID."

Emma finished connecting her laptop to the main screen and took over when Jacinda finished. "Detective Danielson has sent over the footage from the Holmes Park security cams, and we've got a breakthrough. Jacinda, do you want me to—"

"No, keep it in-house." Jacinda sighed, the sound ending in a deep, hacking cough. "I'll just follow along as you all view it."

Emma took the lead, narrating for Jacinda, and Leo remained focused on the footage itself.

"At three thirty a.m., a woman in a baseball cap enters the park with her head down." Emma sat forward, eyes wide. Her excitement was palpable. "Features hidden from the camera. Long brown hair hanging from beneath the cap, and she's carrying three large gift bags."

They all remained focused on the screen as the woman, bags bobbing beside her, disappeared out of the camera's view.

Leo gestured in a circle. "Fast-forward?"

Emma did so, and the trail showed nothing until ten minutes later, when Emma went back to normal speed. "We've got our baseball-capped woman again. She's exiting the park, face still hidden behind her cap visor. No more gift bags."

Denae slammed her hand down on the table hard enough to make Leo's coffee cup shake. "That's our girl!"

Adrenaline shot through Leo, driving him to his feet. He could only pace to the door, then up to the whiteboard, but the small movement helped. At the board, he read and reread the information they'd accumulated over the last few days.

"So...somebody tell me I'm wrong here. We've kind of got a picture, we've caught our unsub on camera, we have hair and maybe a fingerprint...and we still have no way to track this woman down?"

Emma set her feet up on a nearby chair, rolling it back and forth in front of her as if to find progress on a makeshift leg press. "Can't tell you you're wrong, unfortunately."

Jacinda's cough rang through the speaker. "It's not nothing. We're making progress. But we can't...was that a phone call?"

"That's me." Emma waved everyone quiet as she answered her phone. "Detective Danielson, you've got the entire team here."

A moment of static hissed across the air before Detective Stanley Danielson's voice filled the room. "I won't hold you in suspense. Our print is a match to a Renata Flint. R-e-n-a-t-a Flint. She had her prints taken when she started work at a law firm about a decade back."

Yes! That's what we needed.

Mia bounced from her seat and leaned over the table. "Way to go, forensics. Agent Mia Logan here. That's great news, Detective."

The man gave what sounded like a sarcastic laugh, and Leo's adrenaline spiked again. Something was wrong, and they'd celebrated too soon.

"Actually..." The detective drew out his words, tempering their reaction. "It's not that simple. Renata Flint was presumed dead by officials nearly three years ago, shortly after her husband passed. Her personal items, phone, purse, jacket...were found on a steep cliff overlooking the Potomac River, along with a short suicide note. I'm going to text you her home address, anyway, because fingerprints of dead people don't just magically appear."

Leo sank back down in his seat with a deflated sigh. He'd

seen the sort of steep cliffs that ran along the Potomac. If she'd jumped...

"Her body was never recovered." Danielson paused and there was a rustle of paper. "Given the contemporaneous death of her husband, nobody was surprised by the suicide. No surviving family."

Up at the whiteboard, Emma had written Renata Flint's name and now focused on the various pieces of information. "Was her hair long and brown?"

The detective remained silent for another moment, but then gave a halting, "Yes," that left the agents sharing a thoughtful silence.

"If no body was ever found, but her fingerprint is at a crime scene, we have every reason to believe she's still alive." Emma glanced around the room, holding up the phone as if to wait for disagreement, but none came. And Leo was certainly on her side. "Detective, what can you tell us about the property?"

Detective Danielson cleared his throat. "The property went to the state, but it's been forgotten, probably some bureaucratic mess of waiting around for auction. If she's alive...and that's still an if...it's not out of the realm of possibility that she's been staying there while carrying out her crime spree."

"No telling how she's survived off the grid." Mia marked the address on the wall map, penciling in lines between the property and their crime scenes. "But realistically, if she and her husband had any cash stockpiled away and her only monetary concerns were gasoline for a vehicle and food...it wouldn't have taken much if he only died three years ago."

"Detective Danielson," Jacinda's voice broke the air, sounding out above the general murmurs, "have you obtained a search warrant yet?"

"Being inked as we speak." Papers were, indeed, being

shuffled in the background. "Your team can take the lead, but we're ready to back you up as soon as you can get there."

Leo was already sliding into his coat when Jacinda's voice came through again. "Team, approach Renata Flint's home with caution. Keep me informed of any developments. The woman should be considered armed and dangerous. Don't forget she's beheaded three men in the last four days. Well, six. Someone that dedicated won't go down easily. At the rate she's going, we have every reason to believe she's either planning or working toward committing her fourth murder."

Emma wrapped up the call, hurrying to turn off her laptop.

Leo was already out the door and headed to the elevator, Denae right on his heels.

Their very-much-not-dead murderer was out there, and they had a name for her. The time had come to put her in cuffs and finish up her grave-robbing days for good.

26

From my parking spot in suburbia, my view was picture-perfect. And painful.

Samantha Jewell, twelve years old and with carrot-red hair, bounced ahead of a college-aged woman I knew to be her babysitter. She was holding the hand of Samantha's younger sister, Stephanie, as she walked her away from their home.

Stephanie. I swallowed against a sudden lump in my throat.

Stephanie Jewell pranced along without a care in the world, her curly blond hair in a frizzy halo around her head, flaunting her innocence. They were all ignorant of the cruel world we lived in. It hit me so hard...even from three houses down.

I'd come early to make sure the girls left before my date with their father.

Thomas Jewell assured me that would happen, but I'd wanted to be certain.

And that had been a mistake.

His poor little girls would be so sad without him.

Orphaned. Alone.

Who'll take care of them?

Thomas Jewell was maybe the sweetest man in the world, outside of my Michael. Definitely the best of the men I'd chosen for our spirit renewal ritual so far. I'd met the widower on a dating app and thought his kind soul would be ideal for my and Michael's purposes.

"Spirit, soul, body. Spirit, soul, body. Spirit, soul, body."

For the first time since we'd started, I had a hard time getting the words out. They felt like acid on my tongue.

Those girls were so…innocent.

Now that I'd seen them, the image of the two siblings hurt my heart, even though they were safely inside their sitter's car and heading on down the road.

I wished I'd insisted Thomas come to the lake house. Then I would've been spared the conflicting thoughts churning through my head. But those girls were the very reason he'd refused to drive out, claiming the lake house was too far away if something were to happen to one of them.

Suddenly, Michael was in the back seat, his presence looming over my shoulder. I choked on the tears slithering from my eyes. "The girls…"

"Will have each other." His voice was hard.

The taste of copper touched my tongue. I'd bitten my lip. Blood trickled into my mouth.

I forced myself to nod. He was right, wasn't he? They'd have each other. And I wasn't quite alone yet…but I would be if I didn't carry out this last step. Restoring Michael's body. He needed me to finish tonight's errands for the spirit renewal to be complete.

And it had to be tonight. It couldn't wait.

Thomas Jewell's head was the only way.

"Spirit, soul, body. Spirit, soul, body. Spirit, soul, body."

I looked at him through the rearview mirror. An achingly

perfect smile bloomed across Michael's face. "That's it, baby. Just keep going."

My voice strengthened as I continued the chant and closed my eyes, taking power from the words and Michael's presence. I could do this. I'd come so far, and now I just had to keep going. Keep putting one foot and one hand in front of the other, hold tight to my mantra and the ritual, and do what had to be done. With Michael by my side, I could do this.

A glance at the clock told me I had five minutes, so I closed my eyes again and kept my chant going, willing the words to steal the tiredness from my bones. I longed for sleep. But sleep was for the weak. For the uncommitted.

Until I had Michael restored, I had to remain awake and aware. If that meant clenching my hands together painfully tight, flexing my muscles until they screamed with the pressure, and chanting the mantra so loudly I chanced a passerby hearing me, so be it.

I could do this.

Breathing deeper, I opened my eyes and pulled my special lasagna from its thermal carrier. Thomas Jewell was waiting for me, after all.

And soon, everything would be okay. I'd nearly restored Michael...restored him for the next three years, at least.

In three more years, of course, I'd have to do this all over again.

But that worry was for later. For today...things were coming along just right.

I slammed the car door, licking my lips, and managed a little spring in my step as I headed down the sidewalk, winking over my shoulder at my husband. He'd wait in the car.

"Spirit, soul, body. Spirit, soul, body. Spirit, soul, body..."

27

Thomas Jewell gazed out his living room window, peering through the crack between the wall and curtain. His date swayed down the sidewalk with a large smile on those pretty red lips. Holly's A-line dress swung in a way that made her look like his dreams come to life. She was gorgeous. Long brown hair. Blue eyes. Sophisticated. Just like in her pictures.

And she was a widow too. She understood grief, which meant, for once, he'd been able to be real with someone. Even his parents couldn't understand. They were blessed to still have each other, even in their late seventies. How could they possibly comprehend his emotions?

They didn't understand what it meant to lose a soulmate.

Holly did.

His hopes soared higher than they had in the three years since he'd lost his wife to cancer. Wendy'd had a long fight, and she'd told him to find someone…for him and the girls.

Until he'd started chatting with Holly, that had seemed impossible.

He took a deep breath and forced himself to wait to open

the door until Holly rang the bell. When she did, he glanced into the nearby mirror to double-check that he had nothing in his teeth and welcomed her inside.

Her kitten heels clicked on the entryway tile. The smell of the lasagna filled the air around them. "You look gorgeous, Holly. Thank you so much for coming over. I know it was a drive."

She glowed, beatific and radiant in a burgundy silk dress that set off her eyes. "Oh, Thomas, thank you. I'm so excited…" She gestured with the casserole dish. "I hope you like lasagna?"

As he admitted to loving any type of pasta, a quick spike of guilt ran up his spine.

She was so beautiful, but what would his girls say? His wife had said she wanted him to remarry, to be happy…but had she meant it?

He almost caved to doubt and pushed her back out the door but caught himself just in time and spun his doubt into small talk.

All his life, he'd tried to be a good man. A good father. He deserved happiness. And the girls deserved happiness, and two parents.

Samantha won't understand at first, but she'll come around. And Holly…I think she'd make an excellent stepmother.

No, I know she would.

In the kitchen, he pulled a bottle of red from the counter, uncorked it, and dimmed the lights, leaving Holly to scoop the lasagna on their plates at the oversize kitchen island. He'd meant to clear the formal dinner table in the dining room of homework, but time had gotten away from him. Thankfully, Holly didn't seem to mind, and only complimented him on his home as he poured them wine.

He just caught himself from telling her that they'd remodeled the area to make it into his wife's dream kitchen. That wasn't a first-date conversation, no question.

"This smells amazing." He sat and took a sip of his wine. "And you went above and beyond...oh."

He stared at the heaping portion of lasagna on his plate, blinking at the beautifully homemade dish as if the pasta had grown horns.

The lasagna was covered in chives.

Across from him, Holly blanched. "Are you okay? You said you liked lasagna and—"

"No, it's not that." He shook his head, a blush warming his face as he stammered and kept well back from touching the plate before him. "I didn't think to tell you, but I break out in a damned awful rash if I eat chives, throat and everything. I'll look like a spiny lobster and be running for the nearest hospital."

Holly's mouth gaped open, her eyes going wide. Panicked. "Oh my, I'm so sorry. But it's only a few, or we could take them off..."

"I'm sorry." Sighing, he shook his head. This gorgeous woman had gone to all this trouble...what would she think of him now? "Even if we scraped them off, I fear what the results would be. But, hey, how about I take you to that fancy new restaurant that opened up downtown? The Italian one? And you can cook me dinner another night?" Damn...that didn't sound right. "Or I can cook for you. I'm sure they won't be too busy on a Tuesday."

Watching her open and close her mouth, he wondered if he'd just blown the date into oblivion with a stupid allergy. She'd been thrown for a loop. In fact, the poor woman was going paler by the second.

He leaned forward and took her hand, about to ask her what was wrong, when a knock sounded on the door. For a second, he thought about ignoring the intruder, but the knock came again, louder this time. "I'll be back in just a second."

His promise hung in the air as he hurried back up front... only to find his young sitter, Lauren Hadayat, and his two daughters on the front porch.

Samantha was holding her stomach. Tears streamed down her face from eyes turned toward the porch.

"Oh my gosh, honey, what happened?" He bent to one knee in front of his oldest, and looked up to the sitter, but it was his youngest, Stephanie, who explained.

"She puked, Dad. All over Lauren's back seat!"

Samantha let out a loud sob of embarrassment and pushed past him. Her steps thundered up the stairs.

Lauren looked miserable. "I'm so sorry, Mr. Jewell, but I think she needs to be home. She must've caught that nasty stomach virus going around, and obviously it's not a good night to take them out for pizza and games. I know you had plans, but..." The sitter waved her hands as if to say the problem was obvious, and it was.

He sighed. So much for a perfect date night. "No, you were right to bring them back."

"I'll transfer you back the money for food and games and what you were paying me as soon as I get back to my car. I just wanted to get the girls here as soon as possible."

He patted Stephanie's head as she clung to his hips, humming the same song she'd been humming all afternoon. "No, don't worry about it. Use the money to get your car cleaned. I'm sorry you have to deal with that, and it's the least I can do."

Lauren let out a breath of relief and grinned. "Thanks so much, Mr. Jewell. Just call me when you need me again." She looked down at Stephanie. "You stay well, okay? No sharing germs with your sister until she's better."

Stephanie chirped her agreement. He said good night and

closed the door, turning away from the front entrance with his youngest still clinging to his hips. The question of how to tell his girls about the woman still sitting at their island would be the next hurdle. Though he assumed his date was doomed anyway.

Before he could think what to say, though, Holly appeared from the kitchen entrance with a big smile on her face. She focused on Stephanie and offered a grin that made the night go right again with that one smile. "Well, aren't you the prettiest little girl in the whole world?"

I'll be darned. She really does like kids.

Stephanie hopped over to Holly and introduced herself. "It had green and brown bits. I think it was broccoli."

Thomas wanted to laugh at his youngest's constant fixation with puke. His heart beat happily in his chest. The date had started rocky, but Holly's smile grew brighter and brighter as she talked to his daughter.

This might just work out, after all.

28

Emma maintained her gaze focused between the rusted wrought iron bars that, so far, kept them from entering the property, which had once belonged to Michael and Renata Flint. There wasn't much to be seen…mostly darkness and more darkness. Beside her, Denae took the other side of a small battering ram. Mia and Leo monitored the influential D.C. suburb that spread out along the street.

Denae cursed under her breath, fumbling with the ram's handles. "I hate these things."

Emma did, too, but none of them had wanted to wait for a SWAT team to be called up. So it fell to them to conduct a forced entry of what appeared to be an abandoned house.

"On three. One, two, three."

Together, they slammed the heavy metal ram into the gate. The rusted gate screeched in protest.

"Again."

Bang.

The gate gave way. Perhaps, if the property hadn't been so neglected, they would've had a hard time with the iron. But the lock broke without too much protest.

Emma blew hair out of her face, fighting the chill of the evening breeze in a losing battle. She called Danielson on her radio. "We're in."

"Good to go. We'll close up the perimeter on your word."

The home beyond the gate remained out of sight. Only a tree-lined, overgrown driveway curved out into the starlight beyond the bars. A fancy, Gothic-lettered plate beside the entrance declared this to be the Flints' residence. Michael Flint had been a pediatrician…a successful one, too, based on the property and fancy-ass neighborhood.

As the acting team leader, Emma directed Leo to call Danielson and his officers.

"Give him the go-ahead."

Leo nodded and thumbed his radio to open the channel. "We're moving onto the property now."

Danielson confirmed his officers would form a perimeter around the property. Their vehicles moved in as the agents headed up the drive.

Emma maintained a firm grip on her Glock as she stepped forward. "Any sign of trouble, we call Danielson's people inside. We don't take any chances. Understood?"

The others murmured their agreement as they began heading down the side of the gravel drive at a slow jog, two on each side of the little lane. The surrounding grass and trees were overgrown, blocking sight of the residence until the lane turned, and the Flint home finally loomed out of the darkness.

What once must have been an expensive, upscale home now appeared run-down. Tired. Vines grew along the front of the house, groping the siding and brick like brown, skeletal fingers now that winter had stolen their greenery. Overgrown shrubs covered the whole lower half of the structure, healthy holly bushes promising sharp pricks to anyone who dared approach the lower windows.

Doesn't look like the home of someone who likes to chop heads off and wrap them up in gift bags, but what do I know?

Leo called from across the drive as they reached the sidewalk, barely visible through the weeds and waist-height grasses. "We gonna pick the lock if there's no answer, or bust in?"

"We announce ourselves, and if nobody comes to the door within five seconds, we break in." Emma led the way up to the front door, searching for any sign of light within, but saw nothing. The dirt covering the windows meant there was no telling whether blinds or curtains had been pulled closed inside, even when Mia's flashlight beam skittered over the panes. "No sign of movement, but it's hard to see anything through this dirty glass. She could be hiding too. What's the call, Emma?"

"We know what the woman's capable of, and we have a warrant."

"Ready?" Leo glanced around the group, and when the women surrounding him nodded, he pounded on the door and raised his voice. "Renata Flint, this is the FBI! We have a warrant to search your premises. Open the door and raise your hands immediately if you can hear my voice!"

Silence greeted them, and Emma waited for a count of five before she slammed her elbow into the ornate stained glass surrounding the door as decoration. Glass hadn't finished settling on the brick stoop at her feet when she made a second announcement.

"Renata Flint. This is the FBI executing a search warrant! We are entering your home!"

She reached through the broken windowpane, found the lock, and released it.

The door opened onto a spacious foyer full of cobwebs and stale air. Emma strained her ears for any sign of response or movement.

The agents played their flashlights over the surroundings, casting eerie beams of light into the darkness. A living room spread out to their right with a grand staircase rising up in the far corner. In front of them, a large, state-of-the-art kitchen sat abandoned. French doors enclosed the room to their left. Sheets covered the furniture. The floor showed a thick layer of mostly undisturbed dust, but for trails of footprints around the space.

Leo motioned to follow the prints, but Emma shook her head, pointing a finger upward. A top-down approach meant they'd stand a better chance of flushing Renata out into Danielson's net. The footprints could be hours or days old. Better to clear the whole space and focus on specifics a little later.

The four agents moved fast in teams of two, Emma and Denae leading the way upstairs with Leo and Mia watching behind them. At the landing, they peeled off into separate teams to clear the bedrooms and bathroom.

Clouds of dust stirred up around their feet as they moved, and more than once Emma wished they'd brought PPE with them.

The teams exchanged quiet calls of "Clear" and "Coming out" as they moved from room to room, until they reconvened at the landing. Mia and Leo led the team back to the lower level, where they repeated the procedure and confirmed the house was empty.

All four stood in the foyer, and Emma called to Danielson that they'd found no occupants.

"Looks empty, but keep an eye out in case she's on the grounds somewhere. We're going to continue our search inside."

"Good copy. Call us if you need us."

Emma took the office while Denae and the others moved through the kitchen and living room. Aside from dust kicked up when Emma removed sheets from furniture, nothing of interest came to light. Rifling through cabinets and desk drawers turned up nothing but accounting books, old patient records, family photos, and the usual effluvia of a home office. Paper clips warred with thumbtacks for being Emma's least favorite thing to discover by touch.

Medical textbooks and hardback novels filled the built-in bookcases, but nothing she found indicated a serial killer. Or life.

Not even a ghost here to scowl at me or tell me where to look. Nice.

"Everything is maddeningly normal here." Emma's comment garnered no response from either the living or the dead. She moved into the foyer and spotted Mia and Leo examining the shelves and furniture in the living room.

"Find anything?"

Leo shook his head. "Dust, dirt, and more dust. And some more dust, in case you didn't have enough already."

"Where's Denae?"

Mia stood up, dusting her gloved hands together. "Upstairs checking the bedrooms."

Emma climbed the staircase again and found Denae emerging from a large walk-in closet in the main bedroom.

"Expensive taste." Denae waved her flashlight beam over the doorway. "But nothing suspicious. No blood-covered overalls or sneakers that smell like a crypt."

Emma shook her head, sighing. "Just our luck."

Glancing around the expansive bedroom, she realized something was off. Curtains were pulled across a square of space that shouldn't be an outside wall. Emma aimed her Glock and stepped closer. The thick fabric didn't reach floor level, so she didn't expect someone to be standing on the other side, but whatever hid behind those red velvet drapes wouldn't be normal.

Denae came up beside her, and the two women both trained their lights and their guns on the fabric-covered span of wall. "On three." Denae gripped one curtain edge. "One, two, three."

Yanking aside the drape, Denae revealed the last thing that Emma might have expected. A bookcase fixed to the wall.

"What the hell?" Emma holstered her Glock and stepped forward with Denae. The shelves were packed from edge to edge with books about the spiritual world. "Talk about a collection."

Unlike the medical and anatomy texts Emma had come across in the study, these books appeared dust free, but many of them had cracked spines and dog-eared pages as proof that they'd been paged through at least once, if not repeatedly. And, judging from smudges in the dust, in the recent past.

Some of the books were occult based. Others focused on the Wiccan faith. Many more titles were standard in modern-day American homes. Recognizable titles, including the Bible, the Koran, and the Torah stared out at the agents from the more esoteric texts. Encyclopedias of myth, legend, and symbolism mixed together on the shelves. Sections in each book were highlighted. Cramped little notes filled the margins.

Emma wondered briefly if she could learn anything from those texts before shaking her head at herself.

Focus.

Denae ran her finger along a lower shelf. "This whole section is about the afterlife, and we've got recent titles here, along with older ones. A few of these are probably antiques or expensive collector's items."

Bringing her flashlight closer to a collection she couldn't

read in the top left corner, Emma leaned in. But the spines had no titles at all…just stitched binding.

Pay dirt, Emma girl.

Emma tugged the slim volumes from the shelf, grinning when she discovered they were exactly what she'd suspected. Journals. "Hey, look at these." She dropped one journal into Denae's hands, turning sideways to lean against the wall as she perused the pages of another, meaning to keep one eye on the larger room while she did.

Crammed handwriting filled the pages. Rambling, sometimes legible and sometimes not, but oddly focused.

Denae murmured from beside her. "These pages are filled with writing about something called 'the Force of Three.'"

"Same here. Spirit, soul, body. Whoever wrote these is obsessed." Emma flipped through more pages, finding notations that referenced various texts on the shelves beside them, but always came back to the same topic.

She stopped on a page toward the back of the journal where the writing seemed a bit more legible than others.

"Listen to this. 'All the work has paid off in spades. I can use the Force of Three and everything will work out after all. The three vital forces are my answer for restoration, even after death. I knew I was right. I knew there had to be a way. Spirit, soul, body. Spirit, soul, body. Spirit, soul, body. The Force of Three is my answer.' She keeps rambling after that."

Emma flipped through the last pages of the journal. "Half of the words on these last few pages are her repeating 'spirit, soul, body' and 'Force of Three'…whoever wrote this has lost their ever-loving mind, you want my opinion."

Denae scoffed. "They'd have to be to do everything Renata's done."

Texting Leo and Mia to come upstairs when they finished up in the basement and on the main level, Emma left Denae to keep flipping pages while she searched through the shelves to make sure they hadn't missed any more journals. She spotted four additional volumes. Though, on inspection, they weren't so full of notations as the top-shelf ones she'd found.

"So," Denae plopped onto the bed, using her flashlight to read, "we're talking about restoration here. She's gotta mean her husband, right? From what we heard of how grief sucked her under and the timing of her fake suicide?"

Emma, probably more than anyone, understood grief could drive a person to distraction. "Assuming this is Renata, I'd say so. Even if that seems crazy-pants."

Like I should judge anyone for being crazy.

Speaking of which...she peered around the room, willing Michael Flint's spirit to show up and enlighten her. But the space remained ghost free.

Emma's phone buzzed, Leo's picture popping up with a text. *You two need to see this.* She held up the message for Denae, and they gathered the journals and headed downstairs.

On the main level, Emma found Mia and Leo in the kitchen. The fridge sat blocking the walkway between the island and the stove, disrupting the layout and sight line of the space, with Leo leaning against it. When he saw them coming, he waved them forward to peer behind it, where he'd shifted aside a false wall. "Had to do a bit of redesigning to get behind this monster appliance. You can see why."

Denae whistled. "Wowza, Scruffy. Nice find."

"Shoddy work in concealing the door." Leo played his flashlight over the rough edges. "And look at what we found."

A long black duffel bag filled the bottom half of the compartment, propped diagonally so the bag would fit within the hidden space.

Leo had already unzipped the main compartment and pulled open the two sides, revealing a sledgehammer, a much smaller sledgehammer, and a hatchet...all covered in what appeared to be dirt and possibly blood or who-knew-what.

Denae touched one gloved finger to the sharp edge of the hatchet. "If we had questions before, we don't now."

"Should we call in forensics right away or bag all this stuff?" Mia crouched close to the bloodied tools. "Looks like the blood is dried, so I'd guess that our unsub hasn't been here recently."

"Hold off for a second, okay?"

Emma moved over to the back kitchen window and peered out the curtain. They hadn't examined the backyard before entering, and this was a big property. Outside, little more than blackness could be seen, so she opened the back door and stepped onto the deck.

Shining her flashlight around the edges of the yard and a lane that led off into the trees, she found only mud and overgrown foliage. When she focused in on the lane, however...

"We've got tire tracks!" Emma took a few hops down the deck stairs and moved toward where the tracks had stopped just beyond the gravel landscaping surrounding the deck.

Behind her, the other agents stepped outside and scanned with their flashlights, clarifying the scene. Tire tracks were dug into the mud. Whatever vehicle had been there had sat for a while. The trail led back toward the woods rather than around front, entirely hidden from the front yard and the street beyond that.

Denae was already calling the detective, determining the makeup of the rest of the property. Meanwhile, Emma stepped back onto the deck.

"Renata's been here recently." Emma pushed hair behind her ears, fighting off the chill of the cold by stuffing her hands into her pockets. "She just made sure not to disturb anything in the house outside of her secret tool compartment."

Denae covered the phone speaker with her hand and raised her voice. "There's heavily wooded acreage all around the back portion of the property. This house is at the far edge of the neighborhood. There's no road on property records. Danielson says it looks like, from the map, a track could've been cleared to reach the highway or a couple of other roads without too much effort. This is a big property, though. Five acres."

Emma eyed the open kitchen, considering their options. They had to do a thorough search of the property. But searching would scare Renata off if she tried to head back this way.

She waved for everyone's attention. Leo and Mia, who'd been murmuring in the corner, fell silent.

"If Renata is planning another murder this evening, she's gonna need her stash of tools. Which means she'll need to return here to retrieve them."

Leo nodded. "We should assume there's another victim in the making. She's killed the last three nights in a row, and we've seen no reason to expect her to stop. She might even be on her way back now with a body in the trunk. Or heading to the Potomac to dump it where she supposedly jumped."

Gesturing the other agents back into the kitchen, Emma checked to make sure she'd left no footsteps in the gravel. "Don't touch anything else. We'll stake out, and Danielson can call for patrols to watch the river. That's how we'll catch her. If she comes back here or ends up out there, she won't know what hit her."

29

An hour later, Leo rubbed his hands against his eyes.

He gazed out the windshield and through the copse of evergreens shielding their team from the main road. He and Emma sat in one of the fleet Expeditions, off to the side of the back exit from the Flint property.

Mia and Denae sat about a half mile out in the opposite direction from the house, using their Expedition as a mini-HQ. Tucked away the farthest, they'd been instructed to search for anything they could find on Renata Flint via public records and social media.

More police were stationed inside the home, ready to make the arrest, and SWAT units were conducting reconnaissance of the acreage behind the house. Danielson had sent additional patrols along the Potomac, near the site of Renata's supposed suicide jump.

Whatever direction she came from, Renata would be busted.

Emma stiffened in her seat, Leo catching the movement just as he'd been about to shift his focus back to his own research. "What is it?"

"Just want to get moving."

Mia's voice came from Leo's iPad speaker. "Listen to this. It's an article about Renata's husband. 'Michael Flint was leaving the charity-run soup kitchen where he volunteered when a car T-boned his vehicle at the intersection of Siling Street and Firston Avenue—'"

"Hey, we were just there." Emma drummed her fingers on the steering wheel. "That's just a block from Van Der Beek Cemetery."

Adrenaline seared through Leo's system. "That can't be a coincidence."

"I'm not done." Mia's voice rose, betraying her rising energy. "The article says, 'Flint was transported from the scene to St. Peter's Hospital, where he died in surgery. In an ironic turn of fate, this is the same hospital where Michael Flint was born.' The article moves on to anecdotes at that point, but here's the kicker. Michael Flint died exactly three years, to the day, before Terry Abbott's head was placed atop William Rigert's body. All this has to be connected."

Leo looked at Emma, whose face was shadowed. "The third cemetery, Felicity Tree, is just two blocks away from that hospital."

Emma closed her eyes, murmuring to herself.

Over the phone, Denae flipped through one of the journals, the pages shuffling like static. Even though he couldn't hear her, Leo knew Mia was working her iPad like a madwoman.

Leo stared out the window. He couldn't push the "Force of Three" concept from his mind.

It was important to Renata Flint.

"This 'force of three' idea. Restoration. And Michael Flint died three years ago. We assume that the ritual is aimed at something about her husband. If Renata has some wild idea about restoring her husband's life, whatever that could mean post death...what are we looking at?"

"The three gift bags taken into evidence come to mind," Emma muttered from the driver's seat.

He envisioned those maddening butterflies staring at him. Three bags for three heads. The force of three. Three years.

"Spirit, soul, body," Emma added. "Spirit, soul, body. That's got to be related to this Force of Three, right? Whatever the restoration means? Whatever this has to do with her husband?"

Unbidden, the image of his Yaya's best friend came to mind. An old woman named Catriona. She'd been beyond invested in all the spiritual, New-Agey crap that drove Leo up the wall, along with the religious faith she shared with Yaya. And she'd been obsessed with butterflies when he'd known her...

"Transformation!" Leo jerked in his seat. "Everything about this case suggests Renata has a crazed sort of logic connecting all her actions. Combine the concepts of transformation with restoration, and the force of three business, plus that 'spirit, soul, body' concept she goes on about in the journals—"

Emma sat up straight. "And you're talking about some sort of ritual transformation that will...restore her husband's...what? Life?" She grinned at Leo.

He recognized that look. She'd figured something out.

"Spill it."

She was practically vibrating in her seat. "Or his *everything*. Spirit, soul, body, remember? Maybe the head removal and replacement process is part of the ritual...transforming the bodies to restore her dead husband's *spirit*, *soul*, and *body*."

Denae's voice broke through the phone. "So she's certifiable? I don't know if this is going to help us unless she comes back here."

"And maybe she won't be back at all." Mia's disappointment was clear, even over the phone. "Think about it. There've been three murders. Three desecrated crypts. If each of those bodies and crypts equates to one of our three components, Renata could be finished and long gone. That would explain her return of the heads. She's done."

But she's not done. If she were, we'd have found her at this house, or she'd have disposed of those tools already.

Emma shifted in her seat, focusing on Leo. "Remember how we were talking about a pattern...about the recent victims all being known as extremely nice guys? But that doesn't match Jay South and Sid Waller, our first victims?"

Leo frowned. "Right. Which doesn't make sense. If she loves her husband so much, she wouldn't want to include criminals."

"Exactly. I think she loves her husband enough to get the ritual *right*. And...practice makes perfect."

Leo's eyes widened as he followed her train of thought. "Go on. I think I see where you're going."

"Think about it. Morally speaking, in Renata's view, Jay South and Sid Waller were lesser human beings. A convict and a bartender. And they came first, before any other victims. Before the anniversary of her husband's death."

"Because they were *practice*. Not part of the ritual. She'd need to know how much time it would take."

Emma's excitement lit up her face. "And how much force beheading someone would take." How to break into a crypt, what tools she'd need, and what trouble she'd run into.

"So she practiced with jerks...and started the actual ritual with—"

"Good guys!" Mia jumped in. "Marcus Peabody and William Rigert had great reputations before they died. Terry

Derby was a sweet man, and his head went on Peabody. Even the cheating bastard, Rick Royer, was known to be kind and charming, and the whole saving bugs thing...didn't his wife break down when she mentioned that about him? I'd bet Renata didn't know he was married. Every one of these men were nice guys. Special."

Emma licked her lips, her sharp gaze taking in the house through the gap in the trees. "Like Renata sees her husband, who she loved so dearly. Idolizing him, maybe especially after death, as someone special."

Leo thought of those hidden tools, blood-covered and bagged in a kitchen of all places. "If this *ritual*...if that's what we want to call it...is the process she believes will restore her husband, she wouldn't want to screw it up."

"Jay and Sid were absolutely a practice run." Emma sat back in her seat, obviously piecing the progression together in terms of personality and victims as well as purpose now. "Unworthy of her ritual...her husband. So she's killed two good people so far and put their heads on two other good people. If we're going by this force of three thing, then she needs one more. Spirit, soul, and body. And tonight's the third night running, minus the practice run."

"But how do we know who she's going after?" Mia's disappointment had returned. "Renata could be hunting while we just sit here all night, waiting. I don't even know how she'd pick the next graveyard since she's been jumping around."

"But we do know." Emma loosened her coat.

Leo saw her twitchy actions—Emma wanted to chase something solid. "Tell us."

"Michael, her husband. If tonight's the culmination of everything, she has to be finishing the ritual at his grave, right? Taking his head! Find out where he's buried. That's where she's going."

Adrenaline shot through Leo's system as Emma started the engine. Denae's voice came through like an excited GPS guide. "Michael was buried in a crypt at Cedar Grove Cemetery."

Emma slammed her palm against the wheel in celebration, and for once, Leo didn't even worry about her lead foot.

This will not be the graveside ritual you're expecting, Renata. Not by a long shot.

30

"Stop your bellyaching, Leo." Emma kept the SUV tight against the edge of the roundabout, leaning into the centrifugal force. "You want to get there, right?"

"Alive, please." Leo's voice wobbled with unease.

Maybe she'd been pressing the pedal a tad too close to the floorboard. She eased up on the gas before swerving through the next turn.

Emma spoke to Denae, who was following somewhere behind—apparently, Mia didn't feel like hitting the gas with the same kind of gusto. "You talk to somebody at Cedar Grove?"

"Yeah, he's gonna meet us there to unlock the entrance, though he made it very clear that he'd like to go home after that."

"Good enough." Emma focused on the road, dodging around a little VW that insisted on going the speed limit.

"Did Danielson understand our abrupt departure?"

"He said he'd sit tight and wait for further instructions. If Renata comes back for her tools, he'll get her."

All the pieces were coming together in Emma's mind. She

remembered what the ghost girl she'd met had said. *"The lady wasn't bad. Trying to save. He wanted the lady to leave with him, too, but her ears don't hear."*

None of that had made sense until now. But if Renata was trying to save her husband, making Michael Flint the "him" in that young girl's plea, every bit of evidence they'd found added up to present a clearer picture.

Renata didn't consider her actions murder. Her victims were part of a necessary process to restore her dead husband's spirit, soul, and body. She'd obviously lost touch with reality a long time ago.

Mia's voice was staticky over the line. "I hope she goes back home to get her tools before killing anyone else. Danielson and his people can handle it. But even if she doesn't, I'm *sure* we're on the right track. I can feel it. Her husband's final resting place has to be her destination tonight to end the ritual."

Leo grunted as Emma took a turn that shoved him against the passenger door. "I agree. And if Renata shows up at the graveyard, she's leaving in handcuffs."

Emma swerved into the entrance of Cedar Grove Cemetery. Mia, in the meantime, had managed to catch up and followed her in.

A man—the groundskeeper, she assumed—stood by the gate and all but leaped back from the road as they passed him.

By the time Emma hit the brakes and parked against the curb, Mia close behind her, he'd shut the wrought iron gate.

Cedar Grove was clearly in a different class of cemetery compared to the previous graveyards. Winding brick trails interwove between acres of graves. Mausoleums dotted the hills and hid behind well-manicured trees. Miniature street signs pointed to different areas, including a plot dedicated to children.

That's depressing.

Denae and Emma were the first out of the vehicles.

Before either of them could ask the keeper for directions, the flustered man waved toward a stone building down the winding road to their left. The path was well lit, illuminating the brick sidewalks that stretched in a maze between headstones. High-end lights led them all the way to the mausoleum.

Which appeared to be free of grave robbers. At least, so far.

Gesturing to each side of the cemetery, Emma directed Leo and Mia to split off and clear the area. They took off at careful jogs down opposite paths, while Emma and Denae turned their focus to Michael Flint's mausoleum and crypt, leaving the groundskeeper to do as he would. If Renata came tonight, she wouldn't be begging for any gate to be opened.

She'll come tonight. Unless someone stops her first.

Emma zipped her coat up and pulled her Glock from her hip holster. They were lucky the forecasted snow hadn't complicated the night, but D.C. in early February was no more of a joke than icy roads.

"Groundskeeper told me they leave the mausoleum unlocked on weeknights. But it wouldn't matter. She's family. She'd have the key." Denae's breath plumed into the night air. "So she could be in there already."

Twenty feet from the mausoleum, Emma and Denae stopped behind a small group of winterized cherry trees. Within moments, Leo's flashlight signaled from beyond the mausoleum. That gesture meant his side of the cemetery was clear and empty of anyone living.

Denae texted Mia, who had the larger expanse of ground to cover. She flashed the response at Emma. *All clear so far.*

"Good enough." Emma nodded toward the mausoleum's front door, large and mahogany and solid against the dark stone of the structure. And entirely unmolested, from what they could see, despite being unlocked. Renata could very well be inside. "Cover me."

At the door, Emma readied her gun, waited to be sure Denae was in place, then gripped the handle and swung it open. No light shined into the night from the inside of the mausoleum. Emma announced their presence, anyway, and waited.

Empty.

Nothing like the present.

"Ready?" She didn't peer over her shoulder at Denae, but her quiet assurance was enough. In another moment, Emma stepped through the door and shone her flashlight around the space, keeping it positioned under her gun.

"Clear." Adrenaline still spiraled through her veins as she fumbled for the light switch by the doorway and flicked it, bringing a warm glow to the cement floor to match the rich woods and varnish and metal finishes. "And pristine."

Denae stepped in behind her and began moving along the right side of the space. "Groundskeeper said his crypt is halfway down the row...here it is."

Michael and Renata Flint's crypts were positioned side by side, their names etched in floral script that adorned the elaborate plates. "Guess they didn't want to give the space to someone else, even if they didn't have a body for Renata."

"Well, they paid for it..." Denae shrugged.

The door creaked behind them. Leo stepped inside, waving his flashlight in *hello*. Approaching, he focused in on the placards and their simple epitaphs. "'Here lies Michael Flint, loving husband. Here lies Renata Finwick-Flint, loving wife.'"

Denae cursed under her breath. "So normal and sweet, it's creepy."

Leo chuckled. "You and I have different definitions of creepy."

Emma only partially listened to her colleagues as they walked the interior and exterior perimeters of the mausoleum, waiting for Mia to return. Instead, she stood by the entrance and called up Detective Danielson.

"Danielson, it's Special Agent Emma Last. Any update on the stakeout?"

He murmured to someone standing near him, then…

"Nada. Any sign of her there?"

"Renata hasn't been here either." Emma sighed, watching Mia's flashlight bob across the cemetery grounds toward them. They'd move into the shadows soon, but they were far enough from the parking lot that their lights would blend with the cemetery's own illumination. "None of the crypts have been smashed open. We know Marcus Peabody's crypt was desecrated in the middle of the night, so we might be here awhile. She has to show up at one of these places, though…probably."

Detective Danielson coughed on cigarette smoke before responding. "Hang in there. I'll call if we get any sign of her here. You do the same."

On that note, they hung up, and Emma was left staring at her phone. If Renata were out collecting her next victim, they might already be too late to stop another murder. But if she went home for her tools first…Emma had no way to know how the scenario would play out. They'd done everything they could to determine where Renata might show up next, but they were on the trail of a killer who had lost touch with reality.

And all we can do is wait her out.

31

"Troll Friends Playtime makes the best pizza, and we were going to play Skee-Ball. I never win, but I'm getting better." Stephanie flipped to the next page of her coloring book.

I watched with curiosity as the child seemed to completely ignore the sounds of retching from upstairs.

"I love Skee-Ball. I'm too short for the video games still, but Dad says I'll be ready in a few more years."

"Uh-huh." I offered a little *ooh* of supposed wonder when the six-year-old showed off how well she'd colored between the lines of some small leaves.

I tried to slow my mind from racing as she babbled on about pizza and arcade games, wishing the child had simply gone to sleep like a good little girl instead of disrupting my plans even more.

Unfortunately, the big question remained front and center. *What am I going to do?*

Michael could glower at me from the corner of the Jewells' living room all he wanted to, telling me to stick to our plan and "do something." As if that were possible. Our plan had gone down the shitter along with Samantha Jewell's endless stream of puke.

And what would have happened if their father had taken a bite just before that doorbell rang?

The thought brought tears to my eyes.

Michael hissed at me, angrier by the minute. "Babe, why are you just sitting there? We need a head! Don't you love me?"

A lump settled in my throat, mirroring the one in my gut.

Of course I loved him, but what did he want from me here?

Thomas had excused himself to take care of his oldest daughter and get her to bed, adding he might be awhile, but that I was welcome to stay. Which was all well and good, but where did that leave Michael and me, not to mention the plan?

So far, all I'd managed was to feed Thomas's youngest girl leftover chicken nuggets from the fridge, praying all the while that she wouldn't start vomiting all over her coloring book.

"Do you have kids?" Stephanie smashed a crimson crayon into her book, spreading color along the edges of her bloodred sun.

I stared at Michael, where he loomed behind the opposite corner of the sectional. "No, honey, I don't."

"That's too bad. I can always use more friends. I think..."

Too bad indeed.

Her words bled into the background as Michael and I eyed each other.

Sadness had bored into my veins tonight. Didn't he remember what we'd wanted to name our daughter?

How could this little girl's innocence not be affecting him right now? Especially with her name being what it was?

The name Stephanie rang like a chime against my

eardrum over and over. Back when I'd been pregnant six years ago, that was the name we'd decided on.

We'd never tried for a baby again after my miscarriage. The trauma was simply too much for us. Saying we would someday, we'd put real talk of trying again off whenever the topic came up. And then...Michael died, taking our talk of "someday" right along with him.

Lately, I'd pushed the pain away with my focus on the Force of Three, but now the ache in my heart reared back up again, as if pressing me into the cushions to be suffocated. Tears choked my throat, especially watching this child color in front of me. If heartache could kill, I imagined it would steal me away right now to join my husband in death...rather than a new life, as we'd planned before fate intervened.

Stephanie pulled a different crayon from her box, staring into the distance as if thinking on what color befit a cloud. With the direction of her gaze, I could pretend she stared at Michael. My sweet, wonderful, and currently very dead Michael.

There would have been three of us. *Three is everything.*

If only my baby had been born, lived for even a single day, Michael and I could have performed the Force of Three ritual and kept her with us, nearby, forever. Just the three of us. The perfect family. Maybe he wouldn't even have been in that accident...he wouldn't have had time for volunteer work with a toddler at home.

That was how it should have been.

"That's what you're supposed to be doing for me, Renata." Michael's growl was like a physical blow, and I swallowed those tears and turned to face him. "The Force of Three, remember? Why are you wasting time?"

My face warming, I mouthed the word *Stephanie*.

He just grimaced and shook his head. "Don't give me excuses! Finish this!"

I swiped my forearm across my face, hiding tears that flowed freely before Stephanie could see them. "What am I supposed to do? Everything is so messed up! And with Thomas—"

Stephanie stopped coloring and stared at me.

I shut my mouth, realizing what I'd been about to say in front of her…about her father. About the plan.

"Messed up? You mean about Sam getting sick? You really shoulda seen her puke. It was so gross!"

The girl went back to her coloring, and I held my breath for a moment, trying to get myself back under control. There had to be a way to fix this.

Standing as if to go to the window, I told Stephanie I'd just look outside for a moment and see if it was snowing, but she dropped her crayons and bounced up to run ahead of me. "Sam said we'd get a snow day this year! I've never had one. You think we'll get one tomorrow?"

Tearing the curtains open with her little hands, she craned her neck from side to side, as if she'd be able to see snow coming from a distance.

I took the moment to face Michael and speak quickly. "I can't do you-know-what to Thomas in front of his children!" I kept my voice to a whisper, ever aware of the little girl seeking snow just a few feet away. "The plan is ruined, Michael. Don't you see that?"

"Don't panic like you did with the lasagna. Figure it out."

Like I did with the lasagna?

Of course, I'd thrown the lasagna out! As soon as we'd walked back into the kitchen, I'd tossed the poisonous pasta in the trash can and set to finding dinner for Stephanie. My husband hadn't expected me to poison those sweet girls, had he?

He had. He did.

I closed my eyes, shutting out the thought. Michael was

just desperate to be back by my side, the two of us together just like we'd always planned. That was all. But I couldn't hurt the girls. Not Samantha or sweet little Stephanie, who still leaned into the window searching for snow. Six years old, too, just like our daughter would have—

The realization of how perfect Stephanie was nearly bowled me backward.

Stephanie.

Six years old.

The same name as our daughter, and six was a multiple of three, and she was right there…

She came back to me tonight, in fact. This is meant to be.

I shot my eyes back to Michael, feeling them well with tears as a smile drifted onto his face. He'd just realized the exact same thing.

"Stephanie's perfect." I whispered to him, taking a small step closer to my husband as I rethought the night ahead of us. "I'll take her to the lake house and lay her in the garden."

He nodded, those blue eyes shining as he grinned. "The wolfsbane will do the rest."

"That's right…lay her in the wolfsbane, and let fate take its course. And then you'll be restored, and we'll be reunited with our baby girl!" My voice had become too loud on that last note, and Stephanie whirled around to face me, red-cheeked and wide-eyed.

"I don't see any snow. Who are you talking to?" She stepped closer and peered past me into the hallway. "Dad's still upstairs."

This is so perfect. I could almost cry with gratitude. The Force of Three really is guiding me.

"Come here and sit down." I went back to the couch and patted the cushion beside me, waiting for the girl to obey before I spoke to her in a gentle whisper. "Your dad told me you all go to church, so you'll understand. I was just talking to God about how glad I am to be here, to meet you. I think we're going to be absolutely best friends, Stephanie."

The girl glowed, preening and straightening her pink top, trying to seem more adult. "I think so too."

"And I was thinking, with your dad so busy taking care of your sister, maybe we should go get dessert? Celebrate our new friendship before bedtime. How does that sound?"

Stephanie's little lips turned into a frown. She twisted a few blond curls between two fingers before sucking the ends into her mouth in thought. "I don't know...did Dad tell you it's okay? He's not usually okay with us having sweets this late."

"But snow's coming!" I pointed at the window with a grin that I hoped would be infectious. "Even if it's not here yet, it's coming. That means a snow day for you tomorrow, so there's no reason to go to bed early tonight, is there? You can't really be too tired for ice cream."

Though her eyes had gone a little brighter at the mention of one of those mythical snow days she'd heard her sister wish for, she still looked doubtful. "Are you sure? Dad—"

"Not to mention that it's a special occasion. Aren't you supposed to celebrate new friendships?" Not waiting for another answer, I hurried to the sideboard. Picking up her coat, I held the garment out to welcome her back into its warmth. "Come on...it'll be our secret, and I promise I won't tell. We'll be home before your dad knows it."

Stephanie hesitated. From the corner, Michael hissed at me. "You're being too pushy. She senses something's off. Think, Renata. Get your coat on like it doesn't matter to you whether she comes along."

He's right.

Dropping Stephanie's coat, I plucked mine from the closet and shoved my arms inside. "Well, if dessert doesn't matter to you, maybe I'll just go get some ice cream for myself. I'll be right back, so don't worry…"

Stephanie was there in a flash, stuffing herself into her shiny pink coat and grinning at me like a life-size doll. She giggled as she zipped herself up and reached her hand out to take mine.

My last three.

What a magical night this was going to be.

32

"It's nearly eleven. What the hell is she waiting for?" Emma paced along the side of the mausoleum, keeping her steps quiet and venting her frustration through the movement.

Hell, I'd take an appearance by Michael Flint at this point. Someone to give a clue about what the fuck's going on.

From the closed door where Leo listened for approaching footsteps—not that Mia and Denae wouldn't have warned them—he shrugged, signaling his own feelings of helplessness.

Emma huffed and paced back along the wall in the near darkness, as they'd turned off the mausoleum's light. Her phone vibrated and she checked it to see a text from Danielson.

No sign of her yet. APB just went out.

She tapped a quick reply and pocketed her phone again. Denae and Mia were in their SUV parked at the far edge of the lot, where they'd be able to view a good portion of Cedar Grove Cemetery, including most paths to the mausoleum and the main entrance. SWAT members had taken up concealed positions around the grounds as well.

They hadn't been on watch for quite an hour yet, but time was flying.

Where the hell was Renata? She wasn't at home, and she wasn't at her husband's crypt.

With the APB, maybe somebody will spot her. But I swear we've missed something.

Leo muttered under his breath. "Renata's gotta be showing up somewhere soon. We'll be on her when she does."

"There's a location in play that we don't know about." Emma loosened her coat and went back to eyeing the Flint couple's crypts. "It's somewhere. But where?"

Leo moved through the shadows, coming to stand beside her. "You think she has another set of tools stashed away?"

"No, not that." Emma shook her head. "But another space entirely where she can act in privacy. Even if her one set of tools was stored at the D.C. residence, there weren't any signs of violence there, postmortem or otherwise. We searched, remember? Not in the basement, not in the garage, not even in the yard. Everything was tidy, and very much not bloodstained by our delusional psychopath. Plus, there wasn't a saw in sight. Where is she taking her victims to kill them and remove their damn heads?"

Leo's eyes went a little wider as she spoke. And after a moment, he stood straighter. "You're right. The victims' cars have never been recovered either. She might be killing them elsewhere, then using their own vehicles to move them somewhere for the decapitation step. At that point, she'd have what she needs and could take her tools and the head to the cemetery."

"Do we think she's killing them at a specific or random location? And if it's specific, where would that be?"

"Her cliff top maybe, at the Potomac. But that could be really visible, not secluded or discreet. We haven't heard anything from Danielson's people, have we?"

Emma slipped her phone from her pocket and sent a quick text to Danielson. He got back within a minute.

No sign of her yet. Patrol will call in.

"So much for that."

"There must be another location. A somewhat nearby location, too, with space to hide bodies, vehicles, and give her the privacy she needs. But where?"

Emma texted Mia and Denae, filling them in on their brainstorm and asking for help.

Mia called almost immediately, and Emma put her on FaceTime. "I think you guys must be right. If the house isn't her base of operations, maybe she's staying with family."

Leo walked over from the door, speaking low. "She didn't have surviving family. But maybe there's family property? Something else that got lost in the paperwork?"

Mia huffed across the line, sighing. "We ran everything related to 'Renata Flint.'"

Emma handed Leo her phone and wandered toward the crypts nearby as her colleagues discussed tactics. Her mind was stuck on a tidbit that wouldn't come to her tongue. Especially in this dark space, now that they'd turned out the lights to lure Renata in.

So many names. So many bodies...

No, wait. Stick with the names, Emma girl.

"Renata Finwick-Flint. That's her full name." Emma was talking more to herself than into the phone...and that was when it clicked. "Her full name is Renata Finwick-Flint, and we haven't looked into the Finwick name."

Leo latched onto Emma's train of thought. "This is an expensive cemetery. It's not uncommon for wealthy people to reserve several spots in advance for family members, all in a single area or building. Let's see who's in here with Renata."

In another second, flashlights on, they'd split off from each other to search the crypts as Mia and Denae began researching via laptop.

"Here!" Emma waved her flashlight at Leo, gesturing him over. She held up the phone, offering the rest of their team a view of the pristine crypt, blue violets resting beside it. "We have a crypt here for a Henrietta Finwick. Placard reads '*Beloved Mother*' and there are fresh flowers in the attached vase. She died two years before Michael and Renata. Look her up. Search her properties."

His voice rang loud with excitement, and Emma shot her eyes toward the door. She didn't expect to see Renata but kept half waiting for a gang of ghosts to interrupt them. None had so far, but she didn't want to get ghost-mobbed for causing a scene in their resting place.

"Got it." Mia whooped through the phone. "Henrietta Finwick owns a lake house in rural Maryland that sits on a multi-acre plot of land, complete with a private lake. It should say *owned*…but from what I'm seeing, the house was never officially given to Renata. Could be a paperwork gaffe, or the property could be tied up in court."

Leo elbowed Emma in the ribs. "Either way, I think that's our bingo. Shall we get back to the SUV?"

Emma spoke into the phone. "Leo's right. That must be where she is. This is her last night of three, and we've determined her home base now, so we'll head there. Leo and I are on our way back to the SUV. Denae, call Detective Danielson and fill him in. I'll let SWAT know to stay here as a precaution, but I'd bet we're about to get our girl."

Emma hung up and called their SWAT liaison with an update while she and Leo jogged to the SUV.

Swinging into the driver's seat, Emma got the engine

started while Leo buckled in. Behind her, the second SUV's headlights lit up. Both vehicles made U-turns and headed out the entrance.

Denae called Leo's phone and reported her findings as they sped onward. "Henrietta Finwick's lake home is only twenty minutes from the first grave robbery."

"We've found her." Emma's heart was drumming in her chest. "I know it. This has to be where she's doing her dirty work."

Denae laid out the game plan. "Officers are en route to support us at the lake house."

"Got it. I'll call Jacinda." Leo disconnected and started dialing. "Emma, I can't believe I'm saying this, but drive fast."

"Done."

33

I blinked into the night beyond the dashboard, trying to keep my focus. "And what did you say your favorite color was?"

Stephanie frowned at me from the passenger seat. "Pink. It's pink. Can't you tell? My shirt's pink and my coat's pink and my scrunchie's pink! Plus, you've asked me three times!"

I forced a giggle that I hoped sounded best-friendy. "I'm sorry, I just want to make sure I have it all straight. We're gonna be great gal pals, so I have to know everything. Now tell me more about your next-door neighbor's cats, okay?"

And I did want to know everything about her, from her favorite colors to her favorite animal friends and so on. This was my daughter come back to find me, after all. I needed to know everything.

If only I weren't so tired. I just needed to stay awake a little longer. Just a bit longer.

Stephanie's monologue about a cat named Stewie Steverson trailed off as I slowed the car and crunched up the gravel drive toward the lake house. Glancing sideways, I noticed a confused pout on her lips, even as her eyes blinked heavily at me.

"This isn't an ice cream place. Where are we?"

"Well, honey," I undid my seat belt and reached out to undo hers, "the best ice cream is homemade, and this is my home, so we're having dessert here. Surprise! Your daddy and sister are on their way too."

The girl opened her lips and blinked at me again, tiredness slowing her reactions, so I hurried out into the night air and rushed around to the passenger's side.

She held onto the seat, frowning. "I don't understand… Sam's sick."

Oh, please don't fight me, baby. We're going to be such a wonderful family, just you wait.

I crouched in front of her. "She's better. And I just adore you all so much. I wanted this to be a special surprise."

For a moment, I thought she'd fight me…but then she yawned. "Okay. It sounds like an ice cream party. I like those. Then can we go to bed?"

A giggle burbled up from my throat, pluming steam into the cold night between us. "Absolutely! Let's go inside, okay?"

"Okay." The girl took my hand, and I tugged her from the car.

"Sam loves ice cream almost as much as I do. I'm glad she's feeling better. Dad says he can take it or leave it, but maybe homemade ice cream will convince him Sam and me are right about it."

"Oh, I know my ice cream will do the trick." I tugged her up the stairs, fumbling for my keys.

She already trusts me. Another sign that she's our baby.

"Maybe if we put chocolate chips on top for Dad," Stephanie babbled on, rubbing her eyes as I ushered her inside. "Did you know he gets those on pancakes?"

With the door open, Michael grinned at me from the kitchen, arms spread as if to welcome his family home. My heart spun with love at the sight of him. I couldn't believe I'd ever doubted our ability or the Force of Three.

I gave my husband a little smile and flounced my hair for him as I led our six-year-old into the kitchen.

Spirit, soul, body. Spirit, body, soul. No. Spirit, soul, body.

Stephanie was perfect.

Our sweet child climbed onto a kitchen chair. I grabbed vanilla bean ice cream and chocolate syrup from the fridge, staying at the counter to fix her a big bowl so she wouldn't realize everything was store-bought.

Behind me, she muttered on about her family's favorite flavors, but she'd have to take what I had, like a good girl. I hadn't had time to slip any wolfsbane into the dessert, and of course, I'd never planned to use it to claim a vessel. That was always to be done with the lasagnas I had made.

Three of them. Perfect. Omne trium perfectum.

But I couldn't think about how my plans had been changed. I couldn't lose my nerve to see this through. Tonight was the night. The third night, and the last.

When I whirled around, I held a big smile on my face, and Stephanie's eyes went wide. Sure enough, the ice cream and syrup were just about overflowing from the bowl in my hand —way too much for a small child like her—but I set the dessert down anyway.

By the time I'd dished up ice cream for myself, she'd gotten over her shock and picked up the spoon I'd placed in front of her. She looked at me doubtfully from beneath her blond curls. "Should I wait for Dad and Sam?"

I shook my head. A morsel of cold ice cream already slithering down my throat, giving me the sugar rush that would help to get me through the rest of the night's chores.

"Oh no, honey, go ahead. They'll be here soon. I can get you more if you run out before they arrive."

Stephanie's eyes went even bigger, wide as saucers. In another instant, she dug her spoon deep into the chocolate-covered vanilla bean. She came up with a bite bigger than her mouth. Stuffing the ice cream between her lips, she closed her eyes and *mmm*'d with satisfaction.

Across from her, I swallowed another bite. The ice cream really was delicious, even on a night as cold as this one. The flavor brought me back to childhood. In one fell swoop, a sense of contentment settled over me. Here I was, with my husband and my child, eating sweets.

Behind Stephanie, Michael prowled the edges of the kitchen as he observed us, grinning and occasionally telling me he loved me. I only nodded back. I'd learned not to talk to him in front of her.

Not yet anyway. Not until we became a true family of three, all together forever.

By the time Stephanie devoured a third of the ice cream in her bowl, her eyes were beginning to droop. Whether from a sugar coma or exhaustion, I didn't much care.

She glanced over to the window and enjoyed one more half-hearted bite before she peered back at me. "I'm really sleepy, Holly. Can I lie down and wait for Dad and Sam?"

There's the question I've been waiting for.

Forcing my voice to remain quiet, gentle, I leaned over the table as if to offer a secret. "Sure, honey. And I've got another surprise for you too. Would you like to sleep in the most beautiful bed in the world? A real *bed of flowers*? Made for a real princess? A princess just like you?"

The little girl blinked her sweet blue eyes at me—nearly the same blue as my Michael's—and nodded sleepily.

There was no question about it...this little girl was the

daughter Michael and I had lost, come back to me on the very night I'd be restoring my Michael to my life.

I'd have my family forever, just like we'd always planned. My perfect little family of three.

34

Stephanie's steps slowed as she followed Holly out the side door and toward another building. One glance at the front of the house told her that her dad and Sam weren't there yet.

Holly waved her to hurry toward the weird building ahead. It had a round roof and was all made of glass and had lights on inside it. The whole thing was like a glowing white ball of glass.

"Come on, honey. It's cold out here."

She's so nice. Sam doesn't want Dad to get a girlfriend, but I miss Mom. I wonder if Holly could be a second mom? Maybe I can talk Sam into liking her too.

Holly wrapped an arm around her to bring her into what she called her magic flower house. The nice woman pulled her forward through plants that reached over Stephanie's head.

The smell reminded her of the park she went to when the weather was warm. Holly's garden in the little building was warming her up like a cup of hot chocolate. Yeah, she could definitely sleep here.

And Sam'll be so jealous if what Holly said about a princess bed is true!

"Wait 'til you see the magical flower bed!" Holly pulled Stephanie's coat from her shoulders.

Stephanie followed her down the little brick path leading between flower beds, letting the nice lady take her coat. It was so warm in here. She couldn't believe her luck. To sleep on a magical flower bed like a real Disney princess? She couldn't wait to tell Sam. Maybe her dad would take a picture she could show her friends too.

She fought down a yawn, thinking that maybe it was just a little too hot inside this domed building full of plants. But then Holly led her around a little bend in the path and pointed to a patch of purple flowers. The flower patch was as large as her bed at home, taking up a whole corner.

"What do you think, honey? I told you I had a beautiful magic flower bed for you." Holly gushed on, raving about how rested Stephanie would feel in the morning.

But that bed wasn't at all what she'd expected.

The flowers are so tall! If I try to lie down on them, I'll crush them. They'll all die, and it'll be all my fault. Holly'll hate me, and Dad'll be mad, and the bed'll be ruined.

Stopping in her tracks, Stephanie held her ground as Holly practically tripped over her from behind. "I can't sleep there! I'll ruin the whole magical bed, and the flowers will all be gone."

Holly made the same breathy noise of frustration that Stephanie's gym teacher sometimes did when her friend Clyde argued about doing exercises at school.

But instead of throwing a tantrum, Holly rested her hands firmly on Stephanie's shoulders, gripping her hard and pushing her forward. "Honey, it'll be fine."

"No, Holly!" Stephanie tried to shake her shoulders free,

but Holly gripped her tighter. Her stomach turned, lurching as she tripped. "Stop!"

Stephanie's ankle turned on a brick. She screamed out as she fell to her knees, but Holly yanked her back up by the collar of her shirt. The material cut into her neck, turning Stephanie's small scream into a squeak.

Holly was like a different person since they'd gotten into the building.

She was scary.

Holly huffed a very bad word that Stephanie was not allowed to say and began pushing her forward and pulling on one of her sleeves. "Now, Stephanie, you're being a bad girl. Take off your clothes and lay down before I have to tell your daddy what a bad girl you're being."

Take off my clothes?

Stephanie struggled sideways, catching onto the side of a raised flower bed surrounding a patch of tomato plants.

Her palm stung as she held onto the wood, but even when she felt a deep, mean splinter in her hand, she didn't let go. Instead, she braced her feet on the walkway and pushed back against Holly's body. With her free hand, she tried to tug her shirt back from Holly.

Tears stung her eyes. Blood ran from her hand. It was going to ruin her pink shirt.

Stephanie turned and yelled into Holly's face. "My dad says I'm never bad. I'm not a bad girl! I just don't want to kill those flowers. And I've changed my mind…you're mean! You're just a mean, ugly, old woman my daddy should never have brought home!"

"Don't you dare say that!" Holly shook her hard.

Stephanie lost her grip on the wooden rail. Holly shoved her forward. She tripped and fell to her hands and knees on the brick path, landing hard. Her stomach flip-flopped. She thought she might puke after all.

"We're running out of time, and I will not let you destroy all my plans by throwing a tantrum! Take off your clothes and lay in that wolfsbane, young lady!"

Stephanie's palms stung, but she twisted around and kicked out, catching Holly in the shin.

The woman screamed. "No!"

Even as the word vibrated in her ears, Stephanie stumbled to her feet, turned, and ran, but Holly grabbed her by the elbow. Within a second, she'd gripped Stephanie's pretty pink shirt securely, and had begun trying to tear the clothing off her.

"Stop, Holly, stop! I don't like this! I don't want to sleep in the flowers!" Stephanie wailed, not recognizing her own voice.

Was this real? Was she having a nightmare? Where was her dad?

"Calm down and do what I tell you. Don't you want to be with your mommy and daddy? I know you do! I'm going to be the best mommy you ever had, honey, but you have to behave!" Holly pulled at her shirt again, making headway in getting the garment up to her armpits as Stephanie froze in shock.

What had she just said? That she'd be her *best mommy*? That was wrong. That was just so, so, so, so not okay and evil and wrong.

Holly yanked on her arm, trying to angle Stephanie's body so she could get her wrist free of the long pink sleeve.

All the anger and fear that'd been building over the last few minutes exploded from Stephanie in a long, high-pitched scream she sent directly into Holly's face. "No, Holly! No!"

"Shut up, you little brat!" Holly hissed. "Behave!"

Stephanie choked on her tears, pulling against Holly with her whole body. This woman was so, so mean. She just wanted her dad to get there, and then she'd be good forever.

As long as she never had to see this horrible woman ever again.

Fighting, struggling, Stephanie screamed again. She wasn't stronger than Holly, but she was going to be louder...

She screamed with all the strength and volume and weight that her six-year-old lungs could muster.

"Help! Help! *Help!*"

35

With the GPS claiming they were a minute away from Henrietta Finwick's lake house, Emma slowed to search for the turnoff. She craned her neck and pointed when a patch of darkness showed up against the trees. "That's got to be it! Mia, you see it?"

Emma took the turn so fast that the SUV's wheels skidded on the gravel.

"I see you, Evel Knievel. Be careful. I'm right behind you."

Emma ignored Mia's words of caution and covered the hundred yards to the homestead in seconds.

She was out of the Expedition by the time Mia's wheels braked.

Leo was beside her in a second.

"We should split up and—"

A scream cut her off, breaking the air more completely than any crack of thunder ever had.

A little girl's scream.

The sound hadn't come from the house but somewhere beyond it.

Emma sprinted toward the left side of the house. Her

boots kicked up gravel as she ran, Leo right at her side. Somehow, in these moments, they managed to synchronize without much discussion. Emma had never had a partner anticipate her actions so fluidly. And she, likewise, knew when he was going to move.

The two of them skidded around the corner of the home, finding a large, domed greenhouse that was half the size of the home in the rear side yard. The greenhouse door hung open and light shined outward.

With her Glock pulled and Leo on her heels, Emma homed in on the little girl's cries for help.

Good girl. Keep yelling.

She hurried through the door into a maze of plants that all seemed to reach at least waist height. Some twenty feet ahead of her, a woman was dragging a little girl toward a back corner of the greenhouse, clawing at the girl's shirt as she went.

"Stop! FBI." Emma raised her Glock and moved, walking to the left side of the path as Leo shifted to the right and took long strides down the brick path, clearly going for the minor. They'd expected a full-grown man, not a little girl, but there was no question of this child being a victim. "Renata Flint, I told you to stop where you are and release that child!"

The woman whirled, still clutching the child in her arms. Tears streamed down the blond girl's face as she fought against the woman's grip, her sparkly pink shirt torn at the hem and around one shoulder. The struggle had been ongoing.

"I want my daddy!" the girl cried out.

"It's okay, honey." Leo took another step, hands up as Renata's gaze shot between him and Emma's Glock. "We're gonna get you back to him. Renata, let her go...*now*."

Emma chanced a few more steps, closing the distance as Mia called out behind her.

"We're here, Emma. Renata Flint, stand down. Release the child."

"No!" Renata shook her head and moved another step backward. The greenhouse seemed to be a dead end, but she was heading somewhere. Maddeningly, the woman flipped her long brown hair and offered the agents a placating smile, not unlike a mother at a parent-teacher conference. "This is all a misunderstanding. This is my little girl, Stephanie, and she only needs to take a nap! This is all a—"

"I'm not your little girl!" The child shrieked and struggled in Renata's grip.

Emma moved alongside Leo as Renata went to her knees, trying to control the girl's wriggling.

"Holy shit." Denae stepped up beside Emma, gun pointed. "You see that patch of flowers? Those purple flowers? That's wolfsbane."

The flowers were less than a yard from where Renata held the little girl. A massive shiver racked Emma's body. *Wolf.*

Denae spoke to the room at large. "That girl will die if Renata pushes her into that patch of flowers. The poison they produce is aconite, and it's absorbed through the skin. *Immediately.*"

Emma's nerves went cold as she tried to get a decent bead on Renata, but the girl's struggles made a good shot impossible. Another shiver ran through her, mirroring the one that had accosted her at Denae's pronouncement of what they faced.

Wolfsbane. Of course it is.

She moved ahead until she and Leo were only a few steps away, Denae just behind them, and repeated her order. "Renata, let that little girl go. Now."

Renata's eyes grew wider. Her grin stretched into a horrifying rictus that would better have belonged on a manufactured zombie in a house of horrors. "Please, no...I'd never hurt a little girl! I've never even owned a gun."

Yeah, but you own a hatchet and a saw, don't you? Among other things.

The woman tightened her grip on the child, who sobbed louder and fought her grip. "I want my da-a-a-ad!"

Renata's gaze found Emma's, desperate. Tears streaked down her cheeks. "Please, you have to believe me! Let me finish. I'll explain everything. Michael needs me! There's no time for this."

Shaking her head, Emma made a show of re-aiming her gun and centering the weapon on the woman's forehead. "Stephanie, honey, I want you to be very, very still." The girl froze, her eyes suddenly too large for her face. *A smart one, this kid.* "Renata, this is your one warning. If you do not release that little girl, I will shoot you. That's a promise."

The moment stretched out for what felt like hours. From the corner of her eye, Emma saw Leo coil. She was immediately brought back to the cliff in Little Clementine, Maryland. She and Leo had sprung, but too late, to stop a traumatized woman from shoving a vile man to his death.

Emma knew, somehow, in that moment, they would not be too late tonight.

Everyone moved at once.

The woman let out a mad shriek and whirled with the girl in her arms, shoving her forward and away from the agents...right toward the deadly patch of wolfsbane.

Leo leaped in the same second, a blur of speed as he bypassed Renata entirely and grabbed for Stephanie, catching her by the shirt and pulling her back into his chest. He turned with the girl in his arms, just a foot away from the deadly flowers.

Breathing out, he held her tighter. "I've got her. Stephanie, I've got you now."

Emma found Leo's gaze.

She'd trusted him to catch the girl, and he'd done it.

Renata shrieked again. In the next split second, she rolled sideways into the cover of waist-high vegetable plants. Then she stumbled to her feet and darted through the foliage toward the opposite side of the greenhouse.

Shoving her own way through the plants, Emma glimpsed what they hadn't noticed before...a side door, which Renata slammed into, busting the lock, and disappeared through into the night.

Emma exploded through the exit after her. Renata was only a few steps away. Without losing stride, Emma heaved herself into a sprint, then a leap, landing against the woman's back and tackling her to the frozen ground just at the edge of the woods.

"No!" Renata screamed. "No, no, no! You're ruining our lives! Michael needs me!"

Emma pinned the flailing woman.

When Denae came up beside her, the two of them maneuvered Renata's arms behind her back and cuffed her. She never stopped crying or screaming, desperation leaking from every garbled syllable.

Pulling the woman to her feet, Emma turned her back around to face the front of the greenhouse and the property just as Leo exited the front entrance with the little girl still in his arms, clutching his neck. Mia was right behind them, holding a flashlight to help guide the way.

Wailing sirens split the air, growing louder in tandem with the crazed woman's shrieks the nearer they got.

Her ritual was over, as dead as the men she'd beheaded in its service.

36

"I'm going to lose Michael forever. It's all your fault. Please, please, please, please...he's my soulmate! You have to let me bring him back!"

Emma placed a blanket around the pleading woman's shoulders and stepped away. There was no reasoning with Renata Flint. Not now and maybe not ever.

She hardly looked like the perpetrator Emma imagined they would encounter. Somehow, this slight, frenzied woman had been the one to murder three men, decapitate them, and smash her way into stone crypts to replace the occupants' heads with the severed ones of her victims. Her power of will had far exceeded any physical strength she might have garnered from a gym.

And all so she could be reunited with her dead husband. As if that were even possible.

To Renata, it clearly was. Her husband was still present, still able to be saved...if she could get back to murdering a small child, that was.

"Michael, help me make them see!" Renata vibrated with

emotion. "Help me! So I can restore you! Tell me what to do! I love you!"

Hell, she really has lost touch.

Denae approached Emma. "Jacinda told me to tell everyone we did a good job and all that. She and Vance are still down for the count, but I told her to take it easy."

Wailing louder now that the agents weren't fully focused on her, Renata rocked her body where she sat on the porch of her mother's lake house in front of them. "You're killing Michael!" The blanket twisted around her, giving the impression of a plaid straitjacket.

She'll need one. The woman's full-on delusional, lost in her fantasy world.

Maybe this woman will be my *padded cell mate someday.*

That was a terrifying thought. Memories of Penelope Dowe and Kyle Perkins came to her after that, standing in their circus costumes and pointing in the direction of Reggie O'Rourke, the ringmaster. Bud Darl's ghost and his threatening omen echoed in Emma's mind.

"You have worse than this in your future."

She'd seen those spirits, the dead remnants of lives that had been snuffed out by violence. She wasn't delusional, not by a long shot. Just saddled with the unfortunate ability to see the dead and sometimes bear the indignity of playing an audience of one to their performances.

Denae's focus turned to a few uniformed officers coming their way, looking for direction from the Feds on hand, but Emma kept quiet.

She shivered.

The air had turned colder than February had any right to be, even in the middle of the night.

She glanced around. This kind of chill always meant a ghost. Finally, she spotted the sad-faced man standing nearby.

Dressed in a button-down with blood trailing from his broken jaw and ears, the ghost loomed a few feet away from Renata Flint. He hovered over her as she wailed into the night.

Anyone could have guessed the ghost was none other than that of Michael Flint. Pain, equal to that of his crazed wife's, could be read in his down-turned gaze. Actually, Renata's desperate sobs echoing into the chilly night had nothing on his hopeless expression.

His white-eyed gaze slid up to Emma for the first time, and he shook his head at her.

Message received, Michael. She's been gone for three years, talking to nobody but you. An illusion of you anyway.

Emma watched as Renata started to plead directly with her dead husband. But her eyes were on the tree line—opposite of where her husband's ghost stood looking down on her.

Emma's gut clenched from the pain of the situation, the silent horror of the ghost's sympathetic love and his widow's suffering. The whole thing was too much to bear...for him, too, it seemed.

The ghost mouthed the word *goodbye* to Renata, then he was gone.

Renata had never communed with the actual ghost of Michael Flint. She'd been talking to a figment of her imagination for the last three years.

Like the ghostly girl Emma had seen in the cemetery had said, Renata "wasn't bad." She was an incredibly sick woman trying to accomplish something, and she believed her dead husband was guiding her hand. All he'd wanted was for her to stop, but she could never actually hear anything his ghost said to her.

A lump of air blocked Emma's throat, her heart thumping in time with the poor woman's sobs as tears welled up in her own eyes. She understood what it was to feel as alone as Renata was. To have no family.

Emma searched for something to say, but her heart only beat louder.

Behind her, Mia called out to ask if she was okay, but Emma couldn't find the words to answer.

37

Leo held Stephanie's hand as she pulled a blanket tighter around her. One officer had come up with a pink blanket for her from heaven-knew-where, and another officer had pulled a lavender teddy bear out of a bag of them, which he kept for children in need of comfort. Together, the two items had dried her tears.

Six-year-olds were magnificent in that way.

"There was lasagna on the table that smelled really good," Stephanie babbled on, petting the teddy bear in her arms, "but she said that wasn't for me and threw it all in the trash. I had to have leftover chicken nuggets. You shouldn't waste food, Officer Leo. I shoulda known she was a mean lady right then..."

Officer Leo glanced sideways at Denae, who stood listening nearby.

She nodded, showing she was on the same page. They'd guessed from the night's events that wolfsbane had been Renata's weapon of choice. Now they knew how she'd been delivering it. Fucking lasagna.

"I'll give Thomas Jewell a heads-up not to touch the

trash," Denae murmured as Stephanie continued her monologue.

"...and Holly said homemade ice cream was the best, so that's why we were coming to her house. She even gave me chocolate syrup, even though it was really late." A hiccup interrupted Stephanie's story, the last symptom of her sobbing. "I kept waiting for Dad and Sam to get here."

"Your dad's on his way, honey." Leo squeezed her hand to emphasize his words. "An officer had to go over to your house to stay with your sister, but your dad's going to be here soon, I promise."

Stephanie frowned at him. "Holly promised that too."

For a second, Leo's brain lost contact with his mouth, but Denae crouched down beside them. "Agent Leo Ambrose *never* lies, honey. He's one of the good guys, okay? Remember how he let you talk to your dad on his phone?"

The girl licked her lips, glancing between them. "And he rescued me when I needed help."

Denae patted her blond curls down. "That's right, honey. And that lady can't hurt you anymore."

A paramedic approached from the side, catching Leo's eye. "Okay if I look her over? Do you have everything you need?"

Leo stepped back so the woman could take his place, Denae remaining at the girl's side. He admired Denae's patience and steadiness.

Stephanie Jewell had nothing more to tell them, and if she thought of anything else, further details could wait.

They had Renata Flint in custody, and just from what they'd heard already, the picture was more than clear.

Renata Flint's target tonight had originally been the girl's father, Thomas Jewell. His older daughter getting sick became the proverbial wrench in the plans, so Renata's focus fell to the youngest daughter when the opportunity presented itself.

Somehow, the delusional woman even managed to convince herself that Stephanie was her and her dead husband's daughter...after death.

The thought chilled Leo all over, and he blew into his cupped hands, forgoing gloves for the feel of human breath, if only his own.

Detective Danielson pulled into the gravel driveway in front of the house, two squad cars behind him. The area was filling with cops, and Leo assumed the Flint home must be just as overtaken by uniforms now that there was no need to keep their presence secret.

There wasn't much left to find or determine, though. Renata Flint had been attempting a supernatural ritual that involved murder and grave robbing, with the aim of bringing her husband back to her side, eternally. Life after death. Spirit, soul, and body.

Rather than remaining with the paramedic and their youngest victim, Leo peered around the busy site for Emma. He'd seen the way she'd reacted so violently to the mention of wolfsbane.

Hard to miss when he'd all but gagged at hearing the word *wolf* come out of Denae's mouth too.

His searching gaze found Emma near the tree line, deep in conversation with Mia, who appeared dead on her feet. Maybe the night was getting to all of them.

There are too many people around anyway. It'll just have to wait. I can be patient.

A hand slapped down on the back of his shoulder. "Whatcha starin' at, Scruffy?"

"Ugh. That nickname again!" He'd never confess that he actually kind of liked it. "Really?"

Denae grinned, tucking flyaway curls behind her ear.

Beyond her, Leo saw the paramedic actually had little Stephanie laughing. *Good for her.*

"Seriously, you looked pretty intense." Denae glanced over toward the tree line, where Mia and Emma remained close together. "Everything okay?"

"Yeah, I'm fine." He forced a big grin for her benefit and nudged one elbow against hers, meeting her gaze and giving a fast wink. "Just anxious for all of us to get out of here, I guess."

As if his grin were offending the universe itself, a loud howl raked the air, coming from the depths of the woods along the lake. A chill ran along his spine, clenching every one of his muscles.

In that same breath, his eyes met Emma's as she jerked straight where she stood, the same quick flash of terror he'd just felt showing in her expression.

Whatever the hell was bothering him, it was bothering her too. And it was past time they talked about it. If there was a wolf after them, they'd damn well better get after the beast.

Whether we want to or not.

38

With the scene beginning to quiet down, all the techs and officers remained focused on combing for evidence and cataloging what was found.

And Emma had welcomed Mia's company, their conversation just grounded enough to keep Renata Flint's pain from echoing through her blood. They'd been comparing notes, and she was just starting to wish for her luxurious bed, her adrenaline draining from her system when, over Mia's shoulder, there was Ned. Again.

With that white-eyed gaze coming from his translucent head, a garishly bloodied yellow polo, and his eyes and features so breathtakingly reminiscent of Mia's.

Emma's words fell from her lips, gone in the face of the ghost's reappearance—at his sister's side, no less. And here she was, far too exhausted by the day and the night to even consider fleeing from him like she had in the past.

The ghost opened and closed his mouth, flustered. "I need my sister. She's always talked and talked before bedtime. Bedtime is secret telling. It's bedtime. She should be talking, and I should hear her voice."

The ghost was begging Emma to help him with something, even though his words didn't make sense to her. Were these ghosts always so cryptic? Maybe something kept them from clearly communicating? Did they always speak sideways? Emma couldn't take it.

Everything she'd been hiding from her friends and colleagues, all the ghostly appearances and gestures and emotions—good and bad—the weight of their demands, their anger, and all their secrets, pressed down on her, threatening to bury her in the Other, or at least steal what she had of her own life.

This is all too much. Ghosts annoying me is one thing...a friend's sibling begging me for help...it's too much. I can't do this anymore.

A sob broke from Ned Logan's lips, and he tried to reach out to touch Emma's elbow, but his hand went through her. She felt nothing of the flesh, but every bit of his pain.

Mia, though, could touch her.

Clamping one hand around Emma's other elbow, as if in an echo of her brother's failed attempt, Mia stepped closer to her, and spoke low. "Emma, what on earth is going on? Are you okay? What are you staring at?"

Emma shook her head, watching Ned Logan sob beside his sister. "I'm so tired, Mia. So worn down. But I think I need to tell you something."

Mia's grip loosened, lines shading across her brow. "Okay. You can tell me anything. You know that."

Swallowing down a lump of emotion, Emma willed her friend's words to be true...because she was about to drop a bomb on her. Peering around the property, she spotted officers everywhere, but a dock beckoned from just a little way away. Empty and solitary.

"Down there. Let's talk in private."

Her weary steps were driven by the need to get the

secrets off her chest, and Ned blubbered on about secret telling, and Emma thought this was what he meant. He wanted her to tell Mia.

He floated alongside Emma and Mia, shadowing their movement down to the dock. Emma didn't know what she was doing, but maybe caution had to be thrown to the wind once in a while. At least, when it came to best friends and the ghosts of their siblings.

Here goes nothing, Emma girl. Or everything.

Emma stopped at the edge of the dock and turned away from the lake to study her friend. In the starlight, Mia could have been taken for a college student. Her dimples showed around a nervous smile, and her wavy black hair set off her elfin appearance in the same way her brother's wavy brown hair did beside her.

"I'm going to tell you something," Emma took her hands, "and I need you to just...try to believe me. Try to keep an open mind. Can you do that?"

Mia's eyes narrowed a touch, but she didn't look away. "Emma, you're one of my best friends. Of course, yes, I can do that for you. What is it?"

Emma filled her lungs with the freezing-cold air and released her breath, then did it once more. She could do this. She must do this.

"Mia...I can see the dead. Spirits, ghosts, whatever you want to call them. I can see them when they want to be seen. And, sometimes, they talk to me, and I can talk to them too."

Mia's eyes had gone progressively wider, her hands clenching on Emma's. She didn't pull away, though. Only stiffened and stared back at her. "I...uh, okay."

Emma blinked. "Okay?"

A little smile formed on Mia's lips, mirroring every other friendly smile Emma had ever seen from her. There was no fake veneer of support in the expression either.

"Emma," Mia licked her lips, holding her gaze, "I've known you a long time. I trust you. And I've witnessed a few very strange things in my career. Especially around Agents Trent and Black…and, more recently, maybe around you too. So yeah…okay. I believe you."

Emma almost sobbed with relief, but instead she swallowed down the threatening tears and steeled herself for what was to come.

So far, so good, but here came the bombshell.

"There's more. Thank you for believing me…but there's more. Mia…your brother found me when I was visiting Keaton in Richmond last weekend. That's why I was asking about him."

Mia's hands clenched tighter, grinding bone against bone. "You're saying you talked to Ned?"

"Yes."

"Emma…after the night we've had, this is…um…"

"Crazy?"

"Mean." Mia released Emma's hands. "I've seen enough to know there are things that can't really be explained, but…"

Emma felt Mia's belief and support slipping away. She'd been crazy to think the agent would accept everything all at once.

"Wait." Emma glanced at Ned, hoping this long shot would work to convince Mia. "Bedtime is secret telling."

The words were like magic.

Tears welled in Mia's eyes. She repeated them back to Emma in a whisper. "Bedtime is secret telling."

"I don't know what that means—"

"Whenever I had a sleepover growing up, Ned would always eavesdrop at my bedroom door. He always got busted, but he never stopped trying." Mia blinked hard. "I asked him why he listened, and he said that bedtime was for secret telling. He wanted to learn all my friends' secrets.

Boyfriends, who they liked, that kind of stuff. Bedtime is for secrets."

Maybe it's not all nonsense.

Mia shook her head, her face going paler than usual as tears began running down her cheeks. "Emma, you've got to tell him I love him. That I miss him every single day. Can you tell him that for me?"

Tears welled in Emma's eyes, too, and she didn't fight them this time as they trailed down her cheeks.

Ned had heard his sister's words, standing right beside her, but Emma promised, anyway, and Mia's sobs broke open. She hugged Emma to her.

Ned stepped up beside his sister, his own near-translucent tears coming faster. "Thank you, Emma. Thank you." His Adam's apple bobbed in his partially present throat, and for a second, he bent his head toward the ground as if to pray or melt away entirely. But when he turned his blank gaze back to hers, his white-eyed focus was trained on Emma as if holding her eyes on him.

And then, as his sister sobbed in Emma's arms, Ned Logan said something that Emma wouldn't in a zillion years have been prepared to hear.

"Accident not accident. Murder is secret. Bedtime is for secret telling." He lifted his hands to his transparent head. "Not accident."

The words echoed in the air over Mia's sobs.

Emma's world turned upside down.

Beneath her feet, under the dock, lake water lapped and splashed…as if laughing at her from the Other.

The End

To be continued…

ACKNOWLEDGMENTS

How does one properly thank everyone involved in taking a dream and making it a reality? Let me try.

In addition to my family, whose unending support provided the foundation for me to find the time and energy to put these thoughts on paper, I want to thank the editors who polished my words and made them shine.

Many thanks to my publisher for risking taking on a newbie and giving me the confidence to become a bona fide author.

More than anyone, I want to thank you, my reader, for clicking on a nobody and sharing your most important asset, your time, with this book. I hope with all my heart I made it worthwhile.

Much love,
 Mary

ABOUT THE AUTHOR

Mary Stone lives among the majestic Blue Ridge Mountains of East Tennessee with her two dogs, four cats, a couple of energetic boys, and a very patient husband.

As a young girl, she would go to bed every night, wondering what type of creature might be lurking underneath. It wasn't until she was older that she learned that the creatures she needed to most fear were human.

Today, she creates vivid stories with courageous, strong heroines and dastardly villains. She invites you to enter her world of serial killers, FBI agents but never damsels in distress. Her female characters can handle themselves, going toe-to-toe with any male character, protagonist or antagonist.

Discover more about Mary Stone on her website.
www.authormarystone.com

- facebook.com/authormarystone
- twitter.com/MaryStoneAuthor
- goodreads.com/AuthorMaryStone
- bookbub.com/profile/3378576590
- pinterest.com/MaryStoneAuthor
- instagram.com/marystoneauthor
- tiktok.com/@authormarystone

Printed in Great Britain
by Amazon